PARADISE HARBOUR

A NOIR HORROR THRILLER

ALEXANDER SEMENYUK

This is a work of fiction. Names, characters, places, and incidents are products of the author's imagination or are used fictitiously and are not to be construed as real. Any resemblance to actual events, locations, organizations, or persons, living or dead, is entirely coincidental.

World Castle Publishing, LLC
Pensacola, Florida
Copyright © Alexander Semenyuk 2021
Hardback ISBN: 9798750636471
Paperback ISBN: 9781956788112
eBook ISBN: 9781956788129
First Edition World Castle Publishing, LLC, November 16, 2021
http://www.worldcastlepublishing.com
Cover: Boris Bashirov
Editor: Maxine Bringenberg

Dedicated to my wife, Nanda and my son, Sasha.

CHAPTER ONE

The year was 1922.

I was a young man back then, only just starting my new profession as a private investigator.

My full name is Luc Nistage. It's a name that has carried through generations, all the way back to my ancestor from France, who fought in the war for independence against the Brits and then settled in the Louisiana region. The family has remained there for generations, and I found myself growing up near New Orleans. But alas, that is not the place where most of my story happened. This is just the base, my beginnings.

I lived in an old apartment. The family money was split up, and I was given the shortest stick out of all the siblings. Still, this made me stronger than any of them. I learned responsibility, consequences, and resilience early on in my life.

Back then, I had a strong notion of punishing evildoers, and so being a private investigator was the perfect profession for me.

One rainy day I sat on the edge of the bed looking out the window. The water drops dragged each other around on the glass. I had decided to take a week off and relax, but my mind was racing. I focused on the drops and the sound of the rain. It pulled me so deeply into its rhythm that I almost missed the knocking on my door.

Slowly I got up and moved towards the door. My hand was ready to draw my revolver. It was habit, part of my overly cautious nature.

As I asked who it was, a pleasant female voice answered. I cracked the door open.

"Hello, my name is Mercedes. Luc, I presume?" asked a stunningly beautiful young woman with wavy black hair and big brown eyes. She smiled slightly as she looked up at me.

I slowly and hesitantly acknowledged this and opened the door. She was perhaps the most beautiful woman I had ever met, and I was taken aback. My mind was drawing a blank as far as how to act calmly and professionally.

"Are you very busy? May I not come in? I am here representing Allard Van Dausen," she said, her smile growing more dazzling.

Hearing the name Allard Van Dausen, one of the richest men in the country, brought me back to reality. What would he want with me? I motioned Mercedes in and showed her a chair.

My apartment looked dismal indeed. Dust everywhere, barely any decorations, no art, dark colors.

However, Mercedes didn't seem to mind it as she politely asked if I had any coffee or tea. I immediately went to prepare some coffee for both of us.

We sat at my small, rickety table and stirred our coffee. "What brings you here today, and why has Allard Van Dausen shown an interest in me out of all possible investigators?" I asked her after sipping some coffee.

"Mr. Van Dausen was very impressed with your file upon reviewing it. He had a good feeling about it," she said, and crossed her legs, her eyes huge above the coffee cup. I did my best to stay focused.

"Oh, my *file*?" I almost laughed, for I had no idea there was such a thing as a file on me, but I wasn't very surprised, knowing the times. I usually just went about my work, ignoring the rest of the world.

"Yes, your file, Mr. Nistage," she said pleasantly, setting down the cup.

"Please, call me Luc. So, what is the nature of this job?" I asked, and took the last swallow of my coffee. I caught a glimpse of the broken clock on the wall and realized what a dump my place was. No place to be hosting such a lady.

"Mr. Van Dausen will tell you more details and give you more resources, but first, he wanted to make sure you'd be interested. It's about his daughter, Aranxa. She has gone missing after going up to study in a medical school in a town located in Rhode Island. Mr. Dausen wants you to find her." Mercedes paused, looking at me with her big, beautiful, dark eyes.

"Um, Rhode Island? I don't usually travel too far from here, and this type of deal might even require a relocation for an unknown amount of time." I shook my head.

"One hundred twenty thousand," she said, and paused again, looking at me calmly.

"Excuse me?"

"Mr. Van Dausen will pay you sixty thousand dollars to take the job, and he will also provide you with housing. He is willing to send me there as well to make sure he constantly has eyes and a contact there he can trust. If you succeed, Mr. Dausen will double the original payment."

Mercedes grinned, and her eyes were dancing with suppressed laughter as she watched my astonished face uncontrollably change upon hearing those numbers.

"I will meet him."

Mercedes was pleased with my answer and gave me a piece of notepaper, on which was written a time and a place for the meeting. I escorted her out of the building, where a black car took her away.

CHAPTER TWO

That night I sat by my window observing the poorly lit street and sipping whiskey for a long time — whiskey that tasted bad due to poor quality and which I had not obtained legally, of course. Something inside of me told me that my life was about to change forever — or was it something outside of me that was saying this? After so many shots of whiskey, I was no longer sure. I fell asleep where I sat by the window.

The following day I was to meet Allard Van Dausen in a former bar called Golden Milton at three o'clock in the afternoon. It was odd to be going to a place that now operated only as a restaurant because of the ban on alcohol. I got my best clothes out, which looked almost as worn and poor as my other ones. A black coat, an old white shirt, and black pants. I had only one pair of shoes, so there were no options to explore in that department. Before leaving, I sat and smoked three cigarettes to calm my nerves.

When I stepped into the restaurant, there was

no one inside except for the bartender and two tall men in black, whom I noticed both had guns beneath their short jackets. In the back of the empty place sat a short man with grey hair and pale skin. I approached. As he motioned for me to sit down, I noticed two rings on his right hand. One had a triangular symbol on it, and the other had the letter "C" created of tiny diamonds.

"What shall we be drinking?" he asked in a dry voice as I sat down. He noticed the hesitation in my eyes. "You can have anything you wish right now."

"Then we shall drink whiskey," I said.

Van Dausen smiled and signaled to the bartender, who quickly brought a bottle of fine whiskey and two glasses.

"You met beautiful and witty Mercedes. She informed me of your agreement. I chose you after my men examined those who have dealt with missing persons cases. I had two criteria: a high success rate and youth. You meet both requirements." Van Dausen proceeded to take two thick envelopes out of a slim black briefcase he had at his side. "One of these contains your first payment, your apartment keys, and legal documents you may need. The second has photos of my daughter and notes she wrote herself about work and other things," he said, and took a shot of whiskey. "Ahh, this is a good one."

I tried it and agreed with him. This made the bottle I had at home seem like piss water.

"What do you know about the town? I don't even know the name of it yet," I smiled.

"Paradise Harbour. I plan to go there myself soon to meet any big players in that area who might know something. The bad news is that I sent two of my men there when she didn't show up for the holidays, and those two men did not return." He stopped and observed my expression.

I remained calm on the outside while my heart was trying to break through the walls of my ribcage. I started to down the whiskey in one gulp but slowed my hand as I lifted the glass to my face.

"Cool as a cucumber," said Van Dausen. "I knew I was making the right choice. I am also sending a case of weapons for you. They'll already be delivered, as well as a case of this good stuff we are drinking. But don't forget why you are there, Mr. Nistage." His tone contained a slightly sinister warning.

I gulped. "Thank you," I said, and rose to leave. He presented me with a train ticket for that very night. I was in no position to complain, considering he had just handed me a ton of cash. I was very fortunate; perhaps God was smiling upon me, or maybe Paradise Harbour had a deceptive name. Either way, I was all in, and I was ready to find out which one it was.

It was a damp evening; most passersby had umbrellas ready. I went to the station and stood between two benches to wait. On my right sat an old man in old and rather shabby clothes. I watched him give up his place on the bench to a young mother with a baby, despite the fact that his thin legs were shaking. To my left sat a well-dressed man of enormous size, his face buried in the newspaper. The lighting at the station wasn't very good. Was he even seeing anything? Beside him stood a lady. What an interesting contrast there was between the older gentleman who gave up his seat and this ignorant slob. Here was a simple summary of our world, as it could be seen in a basic everyday-life situation. I laughed to myself. I thought how money shaped my world as well. Just at the mere mention of Dausen's money, I had jumped on this bone of opportunity like the most beastly of dogs.

Out of the fog, the black train appeared. Before the old chap could grab his suitcase, I snatched it up and told him I was going to load it up for him. He placed his hand on my arm and gave me a look of gratitude, which made my night and gave me a renewed boost of hope and confidence in my character.

Allard had gotten me a compartment all to myself, with personal service to boot. I sat at the table drinking black tea and patiently waiting for the train to move. I did not want to open the envelope with the photos before we departed. I had some strange and peculiar — possibly superstitious — habits.

Once the train began to chug on its way, I took out the photos of Aranxa. She was a very plain-looking girl but appeared to be studious in nature. I could tell this by her expression and the deep intelligence in her eyes. There were documents regarding the Garrison School of Medicine and a hospital by the same name. According to these notes, this girl was making some sort of breakthrough discovery in the skin care of burned or injured victims. She had been invited to study there by the school. She was smart, indeed. This information clarified things a little. Perhaps someone wanted to force her to give up what she knew? I had to be careful and not draw any early conclusions. I had learned in life that things can be completely different from what we perceive them to be.

It was the middle of the night when the train abruptly stopped. I was still awake, studying and pondering the documents. The black tea was a good tool for keeping sharp and alert at night. I peered out of my window. We were in the middle of a wooded area. Surely there was no station here? I hid my revolver beneath my black coat and quietly opened the door of my compartment.

There seemed to be some sort of commotion in the next car over, but the sounds were muffled, and I could barely hear anything. I went out into the hallway and waited. A middle-aged woman with blonde hair came out of her room in a white robe. By the look of the robe and the slippers she wore, I instantly deducted she was wealthy. Of course, Allard had most surely put me in the luxury section of the train. Upon seeing me, the woman frowned and hastily went back inside, firmly closing her door. I once again stood alone in the hall. My eyes wandered to the window. For a moment, I thought I saw someone running among the dark trees. Startled, I focused my eyes and moved closer to the glass. I strained to see but discerned nothing.

A hand touched my shoulder, and I jumped.

It was the steward. He informed me that one of the passengers had collapsed in the hall and was now being attended to in a separate compartment.

The train began to move again. I sat back at my compartment's small table and stared into the trees outside. Nothing. The blackness of the night drew me in, and as I relaxed, an image flashed before my eyes. It was a face, pale, with horribly peeling skin.

I shook my head and got into my bunk. My mind was playing tricks on me. Staring out into the dark woods wasn't such a good idea, and I didn't even have any whiskey on me. It was too risky to bring contraband onto the train.

I closed my eyes, but then in my imagination, I instantly saw someone standing among the trees. I jumped up and stared outside the window again.

"What the hell?"

This had never happened to me before. I wasn't sure what to make of it all, but it made me nervous. I stepped out into the hallway again and looked up and down. There was no one out. Everything was quiet, with just the sound of the train rolling on.

Now the view outside had changed. There were open fields, and I could see the stars in the clear sky. I groaned inwardly. I had to get some sleep. I knew we still had many stops ahead of us, and it was a long trip. I turned to go back inside the compartment, glancing at the window at the end of the car. I could see someone standing there, staring at me. He wore a white fedora, and the face was barely visible, but I felt his eyes watching me. For a moment, I froze with my hand automatically gripping the handle of my revolver. We entered a tunnel, and everything went dark, and when the train came out of it, the man was gone.

My nature is calm and resistant to stress, but a sinister feeling came over me. I went back inside my room and locked the door. I sat on the bunk and looked at the money inside the envelope. What had I gotten myself into? This was going to be no routine missing-person case. These were uncharted waters of my life, and to sail them, I needed to muster all of the courage and resilience I had, more than ever before.

That night I managed only a few hours of sleep. In the morning, I was brought eggs and toast. I asked for two extra cups of coffee, and thankfully I had no more visions. By nightfall, we were supposed to reach our destination not far from Paradise Harbour, a town called Murbery. From there, Allard had arranged for a driver to take me to my destination.

The eggs, for some reason, tasted better than any I'd ever had before, but then again, these weren't days old and cooked in my old worn skillet. These were a work of an excellent chef in a luxurious arrangement. I was greedily gulping down the coffees, adding just a bit of milk. I even asked for a fourth cup.

As the day wore on, the ride was feeling more tiresome. I wondered about the girl and the two missing men who had been sent after her. How dangerous was this task? What would someone like Allard do if I did not succeed but survived? He had given me a lot of money. I was building a pyramid of pressure inside my head.

At the end of the day, as the sun set, I was pleased that it had been uneventful. Lying down felt good, and I got a few more hours of sleep before arriving at the final stop.

When I got off the train, the air was extremely fresh, and I could see many tall trees around the station. It was dark, and there were only a few exterior lights. The train departed, and I stood there with some other passengers. As per my instructions, I was supposed to wait for a man named Mike, apparently, an older gentleman, who was to be my driver. I waited patiently. As everyone else left and I was the only one remaining at the station, there was still no sign of Mike or anyone else for that matter. On the other side of the station and tracks was a dark forest, and I tried not to look at it, remembering my visions, but I also felt uncomfortable turning my back on it. This dilemma made the long wait even less pleasant. What was I afraid of?

As I stood there, I saw some car lights blinking up the road behind the station and heard some shouting. I reluctantly walked down the steps and then up the highway. There was a man standing there, looking out into a ditch by the side of the road. His car had its lights on, and he held a flashlight. Behind him stood another car with a flat tire on the left side. This man had grey hair but did not look all that old.

"Mike?" I asked as I approached.

He turned and grimaced, shaking his head. "I

think Mike is there." He pointed his flashlight into the ditch, and I saw an old man lying there. I will not even describe the state his face was in, but he was obviously dead. "I only know that's Mike because of the car. I saw it standing by the side of the road. I sent my boy into town to bring the sheriff. And who may you be? I'm Stanley."

I shook the man's hand and explained that Mike was supposed to drive me to Paradise Harbour. Incredibly, he offered to take me there after the sheriff arrived. I offered to pay him well, but he settled for a very modest fee instead. *A man of integrity,* I thought. However, this did not relieve the shock and horror of what had happened to Mike. What or who had done this to him? I remembered my visions, and a chill ran down my spine. I sat down by the side of the road, exhausted and waiting.

After about half an hour, we saw the sheriff's car approaching. First emerged a young man in his twenties, and by the looks of it, Stanley's son. Then out came the sheriff, a tall man with short hair and a rough face. He nodded to me and greeted Stanley. After examining the body, he looked as confused as I was.

"Never seen nothin' like this before," the sheriff commented. His expression was grim. "Mebbe a bear or a wolf got him." He took short statements from Stanley and me and let us go.

Stanley dropped off his son at home, and we began the drive. I had already given him the money. Earlier I had been too nervous to notice his hand, but

now I could see deep scars crisscrossing the back of it.
"I hope you don't mind my asking, but how did you injure your hand?" I asked.

"My son and I are hunters. Thought I'd gotten a wolf, but ended up I just winged him. He bit me pretty bad when I bent down to pick up his carcass. My son shot him before he could do any more damage," Stanley said, ruefully.

I leaned my face against the cold glass of the car window. I remained there despite the ride being bumpy. My mind whirled. It was amazing to me how much I'd gone through emotionally on this trip, and my investigation hadn't even begun yet. Everything indeed did have its price.

Luckily for me, we crossed the bridge and reached Paradise Harbour without further surprises. Stanley took me all the way to the apartment on the ironically named Sinner Street. I thanked him and got out of the car.

As I approached my door, I breathed in the pleasant ocean air. It was the middle of the night, and the only living thing I saw on the dimly lit street was a lone cat sitting in the center of the road. I went inside and, without much observation, simply located the bed and fell onto it, exhausted, and immediately fell asleep.

CHAPTER THREE

When I awoke, the sun's rays pierced my eyes, and I turned away to adjust for a moment. I slowly sat up and looked around the room. It was large, with beautiful, clean grey and green walls, grey carpet, and a couple of comfortable chairs. One door led out to a balcony. I got up and walked into the hall. It led into the large living room, which was next to a small kitchen. The apartment was incredible. Again, the pressure of needing to do a good job on the case seemed to descend like a weight onto my shoulders. All this luxury. I would pay dearly if I failed the investigation.

Well, what I needed first was food. After that, I could plan my day and begin the investigation.

I went down brown wooden steps and opened the door leading into the street. It was somewhat busy already. I walked a block and then politely asked a lady reading a newspaper where I could grab a bite to eat. She jerked her head to the right and said there was a twenty-four-hour diner just another block down.

I strolled there, breathing in the clean ocean air and enjoying the clear, bright morning. In the distance, I could hear seagulls despite all the morning sounds of the town.

In a moment, I was in front of a small diner. Big silver letters on the top read Heavenly Diner. So Paradise Harbour had a Heavenly Diner! Well, of course.

I stepped in and noticed an older gentleman with a bald head behind the counter. He pointed to one of the tables by the window, and I made my way there.

"New in town?" asked a man sitting at the table on the way to mine. "Never seen you here before. You look like you're from out of town, anyway."

The man had chubby cheeks and an arrogant way of speaking. I confirmed to him that I was indeed new. He introduced himself as Jackson Thormund and indicated that the large tall house behind a gate across the street belonged to him. "I hope you'll try one of my group's meetings," he said, without any further explanation. I politely answered that I would try and cut the conversation short. I was very hungry.

The bald man approached me. He smiled politely and introduced himself as Bill Linwoody, the owner. I was pleased to meet him and felt good energy coming from him. I ordered eggs, bacon, and waffles with two coffees. Bill nodded and left to give my order to the cook.

I relaxed and sat back, trying to get my bearings. Outside, Jackson Thormund, who had exited the diner, noticed me looking through the window. He pointed at the large house across the road and nodded to me in a commanding manner.

When Bill returned with the food, I had to ask. "Hey, Bill, what kind of group is Jackson running?" I asked, eyeing my plate at the same time.

"The kind that you should be careful with, young man. The Klan." Bill nodded and walked away.

He obviously meant the Ku Klux Klan, and it made me uneasy. I was a little shocked and revolted. The Klan as far north as Rhode Island? I always made sure to steer clear of those people.

Once I tasted the eggs, I felt almost euphoric, the comforting food satisfying my hungry body and mind. The black coffee was next, and its rich, welcome taste filled my mouth, and its warmth took over my throat and chest. All my uncomfortable feelings seemed to take a back seat as I truly enjoyed this early meal.

I left Bill a large tip due to my deep satisfaction, and before leaving, I asked if he knew directions to the Garrison School of Medicine and hospital. Bill said that the hospital was only seven blocks away, and when I showed him my map of the town, he marked it for me, indicating that the medical school was actually in a separate location, together with the university, Kilkatonix. He also indicated that Garrison owned an asylum on the edge of the city right at the cliffs. He marked it all on my map. I thanked him and said I'd be back often.

I stepped out onto the busy street and followed

the map. With every block leading away from the main streets, the surroundings became less vibrant and more quiet. I noticed the intensity of the ocean breeze. I was closer to the water than before, and once I was only a few blocks away from the hospital, the streets were completely empty, and I could hear the ocean in the distance.

Empty, that is, except for one man standing on the other side of the street. He had a rugged, worn-out brown trench coat and an old black fedora lying on the sidewalk, with no money inside of it yet. I crossed over, took out a dollar, and placed it into the hat. He paused for a moment as his eyes got big, and then he stared at me with gratitude. He smiled, revealing some missing teeth. "My name's Charlie," he said, and I introduced myself as well.

"Do you know anything about Garrison Hospital?"

Charlie smiled a little sadly and told me his story. "I was a big one for the drink. My wife and two kids took out the boat one day, and I never saw 'em again. They found the boat, barely afloat, but never did find the bodies. That made me take to the drink more and more. I lost my job and my house. By the time Dr. Furtikos got me on the wagon, I had nothin'."

Now Charlie played the harmonica in remembrance of his family. My investigator's nature pushed me to ask for details. He said his former home was close to the docks by the water, at the end of Graham Street. I took mental notes, thanked him, and moved on.

Just behind Charlie's spot was a small park, and next to it was an old rusting twisted fence enclosing what looked like an old church. I couldn't tell whether it was still functional. Despite its worn-out look, it might still be used for worship.

I continued on down the street. Beyond four parked cars and a few row houses stood the hospital. At the foot of the steps leading to the entrance was a table with a rain roof above it, manned by a nurse sitting in a chair. Since she made no eye contact with me, I breezed by and entered the hospital.

The typically institutional light blue walls and floor of black-and-white linoleum tiles were the first things I noticed. I approached the front desk. There was one man standing behind it, frowning as he read some papers. He was tall with broad shoulders and a strong build, and his name tag said Dr. Furtikos.

I cleared my throat, and he looked up.

"May I help you? New in town?" he asked.

I grinned. "Is it that obvious? How can you tell?"

Dr. Furtikos lifted one eyebrow slightly. "Well, when you've lived here long enough and seen many people, the way they behave and use their facial expressions...you can tell. What brings you here, young man?" he asked in an authoritative tone.

"I'm a private investigator. My name is Luc."

"Uh oh."

"Are you uncomfortable with my profession?"

I asked.

"Oh no, I'm not, but this town is. It's not the best place for people who come digging around." Sighing, he tossed the papers onto the desk. "Some things are better left buried, untouched, undusted...." Dr. Furtikos paused, thinking. "But I don't mind you at all. In fact, perhaps if you do me a favor, I could be of more use to you? Tell me, what are you investigating."

"I am looking for a missing woman. In fact, she was supposed to work here and had a special scholarship from the medical school," I said. I wasn't ready to reveal Aranxa Van Dausen's name.

Dr. Furtikos lowered his eyes for a moment and rubbed his strong hands together. I could tell he now was uncomfortable but trying to hide it.

"And who is this lady?" he asked.

"So you've had more than one female go missing from the staff or the school recently?" I answered with a question of my own.

Furtikos leaned forward on the desk, his face close to mine. "Listen. Some people just leave sometimes. Some do disappear. It's not my job to be their guardian," he said calmly.

I stood my ground, though nothing in the man's tone seemed threatening. "Her name was Aranxa. Did you know her?"

"Yes. She was very talented. I have some of her paperwork here, in fact." The doctor's face grew a little sly. "But about that favor, eh?" He smiled, but there was a fleeting calculating look in his eyes.

I decided to play along. "Sure, go ahead. I'm all ears."

Furtikos took a deep breath. "This city has actually had quite a problem with missing people. Actually, and just between you and me...." He leaned toward me again and continued sotto voce, "There is even a serial killer on the loose. The public doesn't know, but they bring me the victims' bodies for autopsy. It's pretty grisly. This is truly a demented killer." He shook his head. "Anyway, I had a man in the city who was supposed to bring me certain...shall we say, 'supplies.' You know, Luc, it's illegal for me to give you those documents of hers, but...the 'supplies' I, um, ordered — not quite legal today either. I paid A LOT! Hmm. It's been two weeks. He's never shown up. Would you check up on him for me?" Dr. Furtikos smiled disarmingly.

I paused, rubbing my chin. "Okay, playing a henchman is a first for me, but I guess I really have no choice if I want to get anywhere with my investigation."

"Don't be so harsh," said Furtikos as he scribbled an address on a notepad. He pushed the piece of paper toward me. "Come back when you have something."

You never know where a lead will take you, and I needed those papers of Aranxa's, so I took the small sheet of paper, nodded, and left without saying anything else. Such was my task. I did not expect this investigation to be smooth or to get easier. This town was different.

I didn't want to waste any time, so I found a

young man standing by a car and offered to pay him to drive me to the address on the paper. He was startled, but at the flash of some cash, he reluctantly agreed. He wore an old coat with holes in it, shoes that had seen better days, and a thin gold wedding ring. In the back seat of his car lay a small wooden toy, so he most likely had a child at home. He could not turn down the money.

The drive was rather short, and the driver knew the streets well, making me wonder about what he did for a living, but I thanked him and departed the car without asking him anything.

The address was that of a pub, which actually had a board over the door with "closed" written on it. This was a problem, but I glanced around to make sure no one was watching and picked the lock, ducking under the board and into the pub. The old floor creaked as I stepped inside. There was dust and cobwebs all over the place.

Right away, my heart rate began to race. On the floor was a severed human hand, and bloodstains led to a basement staircase. Swallowing hard to force down bile and an overwhelming feeling of terror, I took out my pistol and my flashlight and slowly descended the bloody steps. I tried to focus on my breathing and stay calm.

Finally, I reached the basement. There was a string hanging from a bare light bulb, and I jerked on the light. The floor was also wooden, while the walls were made of red bricks. It was a mess down there, with chairs, tables, and boxes. And in one corner, there were the mangled remains of a body.

I climbed over boxes and chairs to get closer. The face was nearly obliterated. Maggots crawled on the exposed flesh of the corpse, and the smell was sickening. I decided to get out of there, fast.

As I swung around to leave, I saw the "supplies" Furtikos had spoken of—a box of whiskey bottles. I wrapped it in my overcoat and carried it up to the first floor.

Then I heard the sound of something moving in the basement. I froze and watched the wall. A shadow of something that looked like a tentacle appeared on the wall of the stairwell, and I heard strange squeaking sounds. I kicked the basement door shut, grabbed the booze, and ran out of there as fast as I could.

CHAPTER FOUR

It was still bright outside. I was nearly running down the street, and I am sure the horrified expression on my face shocked the people I passed, who looked at me strangely.

I flagged down a car and asked for a ride back to the hospital. The driver was an old-timer and kept glancing at my wrapped-up box. I had a feeling he knew what I had, but looking at his strong, steady face, callused hands, and honest eyes, I could tell he wasn't the kind to try and cause me trouble.

Furtikos was still at the front desk. When he saw me again, his face registered surprise at the speed of my work.

I slammed the case of whiskey on the desk. "The guy is dead, horribly...torn apart...by...." I shook my head. "Something...and your 'supplies' are right here."

"Keep it down!" He grabbed the box and put it on the floor behind the desk. "Here, all the folders I have of Miss Van Dausen's writing and work." He handed me a couple of manila file folders. "Look, come back when you're not so—stressed. I have more work for you if you're interested."

His nonchalance puzzled me. "You seem very calm about me mentioning a person being torn apart... by something."

Furtikos shrugged and sighed. "Oh, yes. I can see how you'd be upset. But I told you, there are a lot of secrets here. This town is not easy for investigators...or anyone, for that matter. There are...things...that live in the shadows, that come from the ocean. There is more too, but if I'm the one to talk a lot to an investigator about the secrets, I'll also be the one to join the investigator's fate. So, I wish you good luck and to survive. 'Til we meet again?"

I left the hospital with the papers as the sun was starting to set. I was exhausted, mentally and physically. I walked slowly through the streets, heading back to my new home.

On my way, I saw a large poster on the wall. *The Ferry Café. Come and listen to the most magnificent voice in Paradise Harbour: Magda*! The poster had a tinted image of a tall, middle-aged woman with curly red hair and a green dress—Magda, evidently. Below it was the address and the notation that this was a jazz cafe. I love jazz. Perhaps I could relax at the Ferry Café and calm my shaken soul.

As I stood looking at the poster, the nearby streetlight went on. I realized that the sun had set, so I hurried over to get my evening meal at the Heavenly

Diner.

I made my way down the left side of the street. As I walked past an alley across the pavement, I noticed someone standing there. I quickly turned and pretended to look in a store window, while actually, I watched the person loitering in the alley. He or she was leaning against a building, wearing a black cape with a hood that hid his or her face. The face turned in my direction, and the individual appeared to focus on me. Then something began to move beneath the robe that didn't look natural, and I ran.

I ran all the way to my apartment, past the diner and straight inside, locking the door. I sat by the window checking the street, but I could see no one who looked suspicious. Cursing my own fear and paranoia, I decided to go out again, but I gripped my gun under my jacket. I took one of Aranxa's notebooks to read while I ate my supper at the diner.

My heart was still beating a rapid tattoo as I entered the Heavenly Diner, but I was beginning to calm down. I greeted Bill and sat in an empty booth with a good view of the front door.

Apart from me, there was just one patron, a pretty young woman with medium-length black hair and a small white hat. She was reading a book, and I had a hard time avoiding looking at her. I ordered my food, and Bill brought me some tea, so I opened Aranxa's notebook and began to read while sipping the warm liquid. From time to time, I looked up to check on the woman, and our eyes eventually met. She smiled and waved at me. I was surprised and timidly waved back. I wasn't sure just what I should do as a gentleman in that moment, but I motioned for her to join me. To my surprise, she stood up and walked over. I quickly got up.

"My name is Cecilia. You moved into apartment number eight on Sinner Street, didn't you?" she asked, in a pleasant, confident voice.

"Um...yes. My name is Luc. How do you know where I live?"

"I live in apartment number nine, next to you. And I love this diner, isn't that funny?"

I smiled and sat down across from her. "Yes, it is. How long have you lived here?"

As I asked this, Bill walked up to refill my teacup and smiled at us, then winked at me. Cecilia clearly noticed and suppressed a smile. This made me feel even more nervous.

Cecelia answered me, "I have lived here my whole life, really."

I got the impression that perhaps there was a period of time when she had resided somewhere else, but she preferred not to mention this, especially to someone she just met, so I did not press the issue. I did, however, notice a peculiar ring on her left hand. It looked like an octopus.

"That's a very interesting ring. What does it mean to you?" I asked, and sipped some more tea, trying to shake off my nervousness, for I was feeling a great attraction towards her.

"This...." She paused again for a moment. Her eyes grew sad. "It was a gift from my late father—he was a very great sailor. He and my mother left me that apartment."

"They must be very proud of you, looking on from the other side," I said with compassion.

Suddenly Cecelia rose. "I have to go now, but let's meet again soon. We can have a longer conversation. Perhaps we can visit the harbour. Have you been there yet?" she asked as she fished in her handbag for some money.

"Please, allow me to get this for you. And no, I have not been to the harbour. How about you show me this Saturday?" I asked, then remembered the time of day and my manners. "Please let me walk you home."

"Oh no, please, don't worry," she said, grasping my hand in a quick gesture.

I was at least happy that she let me pay her tab. Bill came by again.

"Beautiful girl. You gonna be drinking black tea all night? Not planning to sleep?"

"Just another cup. So, you've known her for a long time?" I asked.

"Oh no, she's been a regular in recent months, but not before that."

I nodded as he walked away. Finally, I opened Aranxa's notebook and began to read with full focus.

Right away, I felt that the tone of the notes, despite being mostly medical, was dark and foreboding. But I noticed an interesting thing. At first, I thought they were simply mistakes, but words kept appearing in the wrong places. I paged back to where I had noticed the first one out of context and went through all of the words I had found so far.

"Harbour."

"Island."

"Clan."

"Darkness."

"Kramik."

I took a break from reading and just sat there, thinking. I had to put these words together; it must be some kind of message. Were they in this order intentionally? Was there an island you could get to from the harbour? Was there a clan on the island? Was that where KKK did their deeds? There was no mention of Jackson Thormund so far. But what darkness? What did "Kramik" mean?

There were a lot of questions to be answered, and perhaps many more would appear. What if the girl had been taken by one of those things I had seen in the boarded-up pub? I had only seen its shadow, but the horror I felt was chilling. That is, what I *thought* I had seen. Maybe my eyes had played tricks on me.

I considered what to do next. Saturday was in two days, and I decided I'd look at the harbour then when I went there with Cecilia. For the next two days, I would visit the university, try to find the local bars, perhaps that jazz restaurant, and try the police station and maybe speak to a detective.

I finally thanked Bill and walked out into the

empty street. I wondered why Bill was not afraid to keep his place open all night. He had mentioned that during the day, his family members took some shifts.

As I walked down the sidewalk, one of the streetlights flickered, and a cat ran out of an alley, startling me. My heart was pounding from all the black tea I had consumed and also from the growing fear and questions I had. My nerves felt raw, and I struggled to calm myself.

I was almost at my door when I felt the sensation that someone was watching me. I turned quickly in several directions, but I could see no one. I peered up Sinner Street into a darkened area where, evidently, the streetlight was out. Though I stared into the darkness, I detected no one, but I could not shake the feeling that someone, somewhere, was watching me. I took a deep breath and exhaled fully.

I cautiously opened my apartment door, and once inside, I turned on the lights quickly. To my surprise I found three large suitcases standing in the living room, with a letter attached to one of them. I swiftly opened it.

Dear Luc,

The men delivered everything Mr. Van Dausen promised and more. I am staying in a hotel called The Hook, located near the harbour. Let's meet soon so you can give me your first updates, and then I can give the information to the boss. I brought a good telephone with me, and I'll be able to relay information to the boss quickly, but he wants all your information in letter form as well.

See you soon,
Mercedes.

So, Mercedes was in town and presumably wanted to meet with me first thing in the morning. For a brief moment, I thought of her in a romantic way, but then I thought of Cecelia. I mentally shook myself. I wasn't there looking for a sweetheart. This job was the most important of my life, and I had not made much progress so far. I had to keep my mind strong and steady.

I began to unpack. Weapons, whiskey, clothes for all occasions, magazines, medicine, toiletries, and more were in the suitcases. I was very satisfied. Mr. Van Dausen had a lot of faith in me, and I had to push myself to the limits and deliver, but I wasn't even sure Aranxa was still alive. That was the biggest question that tormented me all night as I took a very long time to fall asleep.

CHAPTER FIVE

I began to dream, or actually to have a nightmare. I was stuck in a black cell at the bottom of a deep pit. I could hear rats running around and scratching. I felt the cold walls around me. There was no escape. After a long time in this pit, I heard something being lowered toward me. It was the face of a young man that suddenly began melting into the face of an older man. He screamed in desperation and horror, and then I woke up.

The sun had just barely risen. I slowly sat up, feeling some discomfort in my lower back. The stress was affecting my physical state. I looked outside, and there was some movement already. I remembered that I had forgotten to visit a market to get some food, but I did have coffee, and I had picked up milk from Bill's place last night. So that was my breakfast, a huge cup of coffee with milk. I sat by my slightly cracked-open window listening to the sounds of the town in the early morning, slowly sipping my wake-up elixir.

Kilkatonix University was my first destination this morning, or more precisely, the Garrison School of Medicine, which was part of that university.

There was one trolley line in town, and I got myself a ticket after figuring out which stop was closest to the university.

I sat in the trolley station by the window to watch the streets. There were only a few other people inside with me. One was an older man who looked like he'd just crawled out of a coffin; there was a uniformed young lad with a giant forehead, perhaps also headed to the university; and a mother in a pretty white dress with two kids who were fooling around. Finally, a middle-aged man in an old, worn-out jacket, his work-worn hands folded together, sat right across from me, his eyes filled with fatigue, already anticipating the work day ahead.

I looked at the man, and in my imagination, his whole life flashed before me. His poor upbringing, his struggles, his depression. I realized that despite the horrors I'd already faced and anticipated encountering, I was still fortunate. I had an opportunity to become wealthy at a young age. Not many got a chance like this.

At the first stop, the mother with her kids got off. It looked like a nice clean neighborhood. A man with a large, curling mustache, in a tall black hat and a black suit, got on and flipped open a newspaper as he sat in a seat opposite me.

Night Hawk Horror Continues! A New Victim is

Discovered by Detective Robert Willems!

That was the headline of the newspaper. Jolly town, this. That detective clearly had a tough job as well. I wondered if he might be a good source to talk to about the matters I was looking into.

My stop was next, and as I got up, so did the monstrous forehead boy. I was right indeed, a student at the university.

I stepped off the trolley and immediately faced a tall, long, red brick wall. I decided to follow the student, who then was joined by a few others, and they led me to an old green metal arch with "Kilkanotix" written across the top. There was a large sign in the wall next to the gate, which gave a brief introduction to the university and its history. *Kilkatonix University, built in 1865 by the Garrison and Thormund families. Renovated in 1901 by the sons of the founders. Here we welcome you to expand your knowledge and grow.*

So that's why Garrison Medical School was here as well. And Thormund? That meant the man in the diner, the Klan leader, or a relative. I knew I'd soon have my answers as I walked up a long set of stairs and stood in front of the school's library. On the right was a fountain, and by it stood a tall, wavy-haired young man yelling something and waving a paper sign.

"Stop Sut Ni Tul clan! We must stop Sut Ni Tul clan!"

I wondered what sort of clan this was. Perhaps some school organization? As I pondered this, several men appeared and told the student to leave.

I proceeded to enter the library, a building with large white columns.

Inside, straight away, a middle-aged, bespectacled woman with blonde braids wound around her head approached me. "I'm Miss Jenkins, the librarian. Welcome, and please keep quiet. Ask me if you need anything," she whispered, looking rather nervous.

I kept my voice as low as I could and asked if I could use the archive section. She nodded and left. I gazed at the neoclassical details inside the domed room. It was a beautiful old library, but rather small. I changed my mind about searching the archives. I found Miss Jenkins and asked her for directions to the Garrison School of Medicine.

The school of medicine was a much simpler white-painted brick building with a triangular roof. A brass plaque on the wall indicated that it was founded by Dr. Stanley Garrison and was now run by Dr. Stanley Garrison Jr. The dean's name was apparently Mr. Polus.

Unlike most university buildings, there was a reception desk just inside the front door. A woman wearing a nurse's uniform sat behind it. Her name tag indicated that she was Sarah McLellen.

I introduced myself. "I need to speak to either Dr. Garrison or Mr. Polus," I said.

Sarah consulted a list on a clipboard. "Unfortunately, they are both out of the building right now," she replied, setting down the clipboard. "I can see if Dr. Kramik is available. He is a medical doctor and a research scientist. He is next in charge." Sarah looked at me expectantly. I nodded, and she indicated a flight of stairs curving up to the second floor. "First door on your right," she said.

Kramik! One of the names from Aranxa's notes!

As I mounted the stairs, I heard vigorous arguing inside the room to the right. There was a small plaque that said "Dr. Kramik" on the left side of the door. Moments later, a man with a round, florid face and large round eyes, with the name Dr. Ambigo embroidered on his lab coat, stormed out, looking furious. He muttered, "Excuse me," as he passed, brushing by me. I was impressed that someone would be so polite to a stranger when he was obviously very angry.

I cautiously knocked on the door, and a calm, cool, almost sinister voice answered, "Come in."

The man who sat at the desk looked as though he was completely unperturbed. His face was abnormally thin, and so were his lips and eyebrows. His deep-set eyes were dark and piercing. I introduced myself.

"What can I do for you today...you said your name is Luc? Private investigator?" He paused and smiled slightly. "Has someone been murdered? Now that would be a shocker in this town."

"I'm actually investigating a missing person case. Aranxa Van Dausen. Did you know her?"

"Oh yes, but excuse me for a moment. I must use the restroom." He nodded and left the room. Dr.

Kramik seemed calm at the mention of Aranxa's name.

I looked around the room. There were many strange drawings on the walls, which I did not understand. On one of the small tables lay the skull of a goat, and on another the skull of a human.

"So yes...." I heard his voice and turned. Kramik sat down in his office chair. "I knew her—arrogant, rich braaat." He stretched the word out and chuckled. "Those things, even coupled with a lot of talent, can cause you to make some dangerous enemies in this town. And besides, have you heard of our serial killer? A mastermind. Night Hawk, they call him. Some of his victims are found in such shape that there is no way to identify them. Maybe your Miss Van Dausen was careless one night."

Kramik certainly didn't think much of his fellow human beings, a strange trait in a doctor. "We shouldn't blame the victims, I think. Do you have any papers of hers? Anything specific that could help me?" The man's demeanor was unsettling.

"No," he said, lighting a cigarette with a large gold lighter. Kramik took a long draw on the cigarette and blew a geyser of smoke toward the ceiling. "You should file a report and speak to our detective, Robert Willems. He's quite an annoying character himself. Maybe you'll find him amusing. Well, I have to get back to work." Obviously, he was giving me nothing further.

I thanked Kramik for his time and left, but I knew without any doubt that he was hiding something, and the feeling I got from him was not good. I had to make sure to watch this man at night. For the moment, I decided that going to the police station was actually a good idea indeed and part of my plan.

But my stomach growled, and a wave of low energy hit me. I entered the very first eatery I saw, DV's. It was even more spare than the Heavenly Diner. With only a few people inside, I got my order of a sandwich and a coffee quickly. The food was quite satisfactory despite being very simple. I found the police station on my map and decided to walk there, as it wasn't far from the university. I decided to forego transportation and give my legs some exercise.

As I walked across the street, I heard the familiar sound of a harmonica. I turned my head, and there at the corner was Charlie. I remembered then that I also had to investigate his story, but that would have to wait for another time. I walked up to him, and his eyes sparkled as he saw me. I warmly greeted him and dropped a dollar into his hat. He thanked me sincerely and said he was very hungry, and he now had enough cash to get a few things at the market. That reminded me that I needed to do some shopping as well. Charlie said there was a store nearby and pointed to it on my map. Fortunately, it was on the way to the police station. This was perfect. Get groceries, try to find that Detective Willems, then go and rest at home. The day was going almost too well. I hoped it would continue to roll on smoothly. I shook Charlie's hand and continued on my way.

I turned into a street which was a shortcut judging from the map, but what I saw was an old abandoned trolley with its red paint peeling. There were a few homeless men seated against a brick wall. I walked past the trolley. The street was long, and I saw no one else ahead, just old buildings that appeared to be abandoned. I proceeded with caution, carefully checking every corner and side alley. On one of the old broken doors, I saw "Sut Ni Tul" written in white paint. I remembered the young man yelling about it. I was hesitant to check it out, but curiosity overpowered me, and I pushed on the door. It gave in immediately, falling to the floor and raising a clout of dust.

It was pretty dark, and I couldn't really see anything of note, but I was startled by a sound in a corner. I swiftly drew my pistol, and a homeless man curled in the corner cowered and yelled, "Don't shoot!" I holstered the pistol and wondered how he had gotten into the house, and I noticed a large hole in the wall, partially covered by an old quilt.

"Hey, you, calm down. What is Sut Ni Tul?" I asked him calmly.

"I dunno, some club? Go to the Dark Turtle and ask. They used to have members of it goin' in there, but, well...since so many murders in these parts, I don't know nothing about it anymore."

"Murders?"

"The Night Hawk kills a lot around here, sir. Coppers don't care about people here." The man lifted a bottle wrapped in a paper bag to his lips.

"What's the Dark Turtle?"

"It's a bar at the end of the street, right on the water canal."

I thanked him and left the house. I shouldn't have taken this detour, but now I had to check further, so I sped up my steps to get to the Dark Turtle.

This was certainly not the best part of town. Mist was coming in off the water, and farther ahead, there was a group of men, clearly drunk, wearing ragged clothes, yelling and throwing things. To my left, I saw a sign that read "Golden Books." In spite of the rundown street, this bookstore was actually open, and to avoid the men, I stepped inside.

It was a surprisingly cozy and neat establishment. Most of the walls and shelves were made out of dark brown wood, and the floor was covered with a deep, dark green carpet. A bell had rung when I entered the store, and from behind the shelves, I heard a rich, hearty, "Welcome!" I made my way around the shelves and came upon a man sitting at a black desk. A table lamp made a pool of light on the desktop, and an open book sat in front of the man.

His voice did not fit his frame at all. The man had long black hair, a sharp nose, and rather small green eyes, but the most unusual thing about his visage was a long thin scar running down the left side of his face from his temple to his chin. I tried not to stare at the scar.

"I'm Kasp Nudd, the owner of this store. Do you like books?" he asked, and placed a bookmark in the open book and closed it. I read the title upside down. *Dark Rituals*. Great.

"My name is Luc. And yes, I like books. But— aren't you concerned, running a business in this part of town?"

"Worried?" He chuckled. "Turn around." He pointed behind me.

I turned and saw a large glass cabinet. It showcased a uniform from the Great War adorned with many medals.

"Anyone who messes with me in these parts should be worried...not me. And they all know it."

"But how about this killer I have heard about? Night Hawk?"

Nudd shrugged and gave a smile that softened his looks considerably. "Night Hawk is not a problem for me. Is there anything, in particular, you are looking for?"

Sometimes you have to go down the path that's in front of you. "I'll be honest with you, Kasp. I want to know more about what Sut Ni Tul means, and I'm looking for a missing young lady."

"Ah, now we're talking." Nudd sat back in his chair and folded his hands over his stomach, which was covered by a striped vest with a watch chain and fob. "The Sut Ni Tul clan. They're demon worshipers, Luc. They worship a sea creature, a monster. They have dark priests who conduct rituals on people. I'm learning more about them. Reading a lot about old rituals and pagan practices." He looked at me piercingly. "There

is only one way to deal with such evil. You be careful...
and maybe we can help each other eventually."

I was puzzled and intrigued. "How so, Kasp?"

"I want this clan gone from Paradise Harbour,
and you are looking for a missing woman. You
understand? We can help each other."

"But what is your plan?"

He gave a weak smile. "It's simple. Find them,
kill them," he answered.

Not quite the answer I expected. Was Kasp
Nudd crazy? "Oh...I think that might not be the route
I'll have to take."

"You think that now, Luc, but soon you'll be
back, and you'll see that I am a man who can help you
and maybe even save you. Good luck." He reached for
his book.

I looked out the window and saw that the street
was clear. I thanked Kasp Nudd and left.

As the homeless man had told me, at the end
of the street, I found the canal with a dock and a bar
with a sign saying The Dark Turtle right next to it. I
was pondering what Kasp had told me and figured
I'd better not discount anything, especially after all I'd
seen. I decided I'd try to get out of this neighborhood
and head home after visiting the Dark Turtle, so I
wouldn't end up in this area when darkness fell.

I entered through the doors, and to my surprise,
the place was quite bright. The walls were white, and
the bar, tables, and chairs were made of light-colored
wood. Behind the bar stood a middle-aged man. At the

bar stood another man, a bit stocky with a red face, clearly drunk, and one waitress was organizing the tables. There was no one else inside. Obviously, the Prohibition rules didn't apply here, and as I already knew, the police didn't care much for this area, so a drunkard wasn't a surprise at all.

I approached the bar and sat on a stool.

"What will it be?" asked the man.

"Beer?" I asked hesitantly.

"One coming up."

"What's your name? Are you the owner?"

"I'm John, and yes, Dark Turtle is mine."

"I saw the sign—it says you're open all night?"

"Yeah, I live upstairs, so does Maria." He pointed at the waitress. "She helps when I need a nap, and sometimes my brother does too. Actually, he's napping now."

"You're not worried about the neighborhood?"

"Why? All the crazy crap happens outside, not in here. I always stay inside at night. You should too. You're obviously new around here. The coppers don't care to come around here neither. No one to fear as long as I stay indoors." He placed a beer in front of me.

"Ahh, smells good." I took a sip. "Tastes great too. Been a while since I had one."

"Great, glad you like it...um...."

"Luc."

"Good, good. Welcome, Luc."

"So, what do you think about the killings? Any suspects? Have you seen strange men here?"

"Hahaha!" John threw back his head and laughed heartily. "Strange men are all I get in here! You're strange too!"

I smiled; he was right, indeed. "I'm actually a private investigator. Looking for a missing woman."

"Oh boy, lots of 'strange men' in these parts, 'specially with that clan around. They used to come in here and eye Maria as well, but I shot one of 'em, and they stopped coming, and then the Night Hawk started killing 'em. Not as many of them around here anymore."

"Wait.... Night Hawk, he kills anyone, right?"

"That's what the papers write, that's what the top men spread, but here we know he hunts members of that freaky Sut Ni Tul clan, and *the* Klan too...you know what I mean?"

"Wow...."

I paused for a moment, thinking about it. So this serial killer, he must have some kind of a vendetta against these groups.

"Don't think about too much, man. Who's the missing lady you're looking for?"

"Her name is Aranxa. She was a medical student at the university."

"Sorry, never heard such a name in my life. This is a first. Hope you find her—alive."

I nodded and drank more beer. My biggest fear, the thought that dogged me constantly, was finding her dead.

"Young girls go missing mostly in the rich

harbour parts." I heard a female voice behind me. It was the waitress, Maria.

"How come?"

Maria hunched her shoulders. "That's just how it is. John Haster, Mitch Stochild, Marie Toussant. Those are the big names. They live around there, and they run this city. Thormund, too, I suppose." She finished and went back to setting another table.

"Maria is no ordinary girl, Luc. She's got a degree, used to work for a newspaper. Used to work at Paradise Times under Clara Binton. Largest newspaper in the area. Some friends of hers went missing. When the newspaper tried to dig, Clara was threatened, and Maria was fired. Since then, the paper doesn't dig anymore on those people, but maybe Clara could tell you something in private?"

"Indeed... Hmm." I was glad I'd made this detour. I took out my notebook and jotted down the names. I'd have to do some research.

CHAPTER SIX

Feeling just a little buzzed from the beer, I thanked John and Maria and went out. I was surprised at how fast the time had passed. It was still bright out, but it would not be for long. The sun was starting to set, and I hurried to a trolley stop, which John had kindly indicated for me.

On the way back, I passed Golden Books again. I had so much on my mind. Kasp Nudd was an interesting character, and something told me that he was indeed correct about me coming back. I got out of the neighborhood and onto the trolley just in time for nightfall. Luckily there was a stop just a block away from my apartment. I relaxed into the seat and decided not to observe the passengers this time; I'd just stare out of the window.

As the streets went by one by one, suddenly I saw something that made my heart lurch in terror. I saw a man in an alley wearing a hood, with what looked like tentacles trailing behind him in the shadows. I blinked hard and found myself saying a silent prayer. Oh God, was it just my fatigued mind and the alcohol?

I took a deep breath. The train, then that place the doctor sent me to, and the nighttime walk. I had been seeing too many "visions." Perhaps it was reality, or maybe I was just a madman who was able to simply put on an act around others of being normal without even knowing it. Oh, I was getting myself tangled. I closed my eyes and focused on my breathing. I continued until my stop, and when I got off, I was feeling calm and more like myself, but also aware that the night was not yet over as I began my walk towards Bill's diner.

I kept looking over my shoulder and from side to side. I was startled by a man who came out of a side street, and I almost bumped into him. He looked at me as though I were crazy and shook his head as he strode away. I entered the diner and sat down, still trying to conquer the fear.

Bill came up to me, after serving a couple in the corner of the diner, and took my order. He looked more tired than he had on previous days. I ate my meal and was honestly out of there pretty quickly, as I had to do my best to get a good rest and begin to gather information on all the names I'd gotten that day.

That night I slept well, and in the morning, I felt refreshed. I dedicated the day to boring research, gathering documents in the town hall archives, the university library, and some files that Allard had sent in one of the suitcases. Later in the day, I went over to the *Paradise Times* newspaper to check their archives as well.

In reception, I was met by a pretty dark-skinned lady with a beautiful smile — Clara Binton. She was excited to know I was a private investigator and agreed to let me check the archives on the condition that I'd help her with some field research for future publication. I agreed but made no mention of the subjects I'd heard of in the Dark Turtle. I wanted to wait until after I looked into the archives; otherwise, if the subject was something she wanted to hide, she could deny my access to them, and I'd get nowhere.

When alone in the archives room, I opened the "unpublished" section and began quickly looking over the titles. I found two papers containing the names of Mitch Stochild, Marie Toussant, and John Hastor, together with missing young women. However, there weren't many specifics, and the articles were unfinished. I had to speak to Clara.

"Say, Clara, do you have some time for a coffee and conversation?" I asked when I entered her office.

Clara smiled happily and motioned for me to sit down. Her office was cozy, with a beautiful desk and nice chairs. She left and returned with a pot of warmed-up coffee she'd made earlier, but she had no milk for me, so I had to drink it black.

We sipped in silence for a few minutes, then I began. "Clara, I spoke to a friend of yours, or perhaps a past colleague. Maria." I stopped to see her reaction. Clara looked down into her cup for a moment. She seemed sad.

"And?" she said finally.

"Maria said that you could possibly help me regarding some young women's disappearances. No one will know you gave me the information, I promise."

Clara sipped her coffee and waited a minute, thinking. Then she got up and closed the office door. "I do want to see justice...," she finally spoke. "But I doubt in this town that'll ever be possible."

I asked her about the strange things I'd seen.

Clara shook her head. A puzzled frown creased her pretty features. "I have heard many rumors and stories about strange things here, but no one ever seems to have any facts or evidence. There are certain things that even my reporters steer clear of."

Remembering Aranxa's notes, I asked if there were an island off the coast.

"Yes, there is," Clara confirmed, "but there is nothing there and no commercial travel to it." She continued by telling me details about several individuals and their dealings. I took notes.

Once I was back in my apartment, it was time to put it all together. Mitch Stochild was an incredibly wealthy businessman. He was also involved in the illegal sales of alcohol. He had a strong connection to the missing girls and to the Sut Ni Tul clan, leading me to speculate that the two were linked somehow. He was also a sponsor of the Manland gang, run by Ante Manland.

John Haster was the owner of the biggest bank in

the region. He had a strong connection to prostitution. He was the sponsor of the Fullstrom gang, run by Tom Fullstrom.

Marie Toussant, an opium magnate, was also known as "Lady Death." It looked as though she ran a house of prostitution.

Apparently, the shady professor and Doctor Kramik, whom I had met, were working for Mitch Stochild.

Clara had told me that the detective Robert Willems was honest but struggling and that the Chief of Police, Sam Stolz, was controlled by John Haster. "Also," Clara had said to me, her eyes enormous, "Willems revealed to me that the Night Hawk carves letters into his victims. We have not put this information out to the public." So that was one thing Willems kept back to discourage and reveal, copycat killers.

She also mentioned an old professor, Gideon Slid, who spent his life studying various clans and worshippers. Clara advised me to seek him out as well.

Clara did not know much about Kasp Nudd, except that he was a war hero. And she said Thormund was too preoccupied with KKK business and his own ego to be worried about taking more control from the other three.

My head was spinning as I sat at my table, analyzing all of the notes and trying to remember all of the names. Tomorrow I was going to go out with my beautiful and enchanting neighbor, Cecilia, and that was something to think about. I also had to check in with Mercedes. I decided that would be all for today, to give my mind a break and continue with a more full day of investigation in the morning.

I put everything away and sat by the window with tea and whiskey. I watched the dimly illuminated street, expecting to see something horrible, but nothing of that sort happened this time.

Once again, I dreamed of people's faces peeling, of strange creatures coming from the waters, and woke up with a sense of horror—and much too early.

I cooked some eggs, which I had finally picked up at the market the day before, and coffee. I sat by the window and watched the street slowly come more and more alive. Then at about nine, I heard a knock on my door. When I opened it, it was a surprise to see Cecilia standing there wearing a pretty light pink dress.

"I thought you might like to go out early," she said, tilting her head in its pink straw cloche. I was embarrassed since I had yet to bathe and shave and asked her to wait on the couch while I got ready. She laughed and gracefully sat on the sofa. I hurried and got myself in order, putting on the best suit Dausen had sent me.

She gave me her hand, and once on the street, we got a cab to ride to the harbour. I felt lucky, as cabs were a rarity in this town. I had hardly seen any since I'd arrived.

The drive was slow, as many people were out on this beautiful Saturday and kept crossing the street anywhere and everywhere. Some even walked on the road, testing our driver's patience—and he did not seem the patient type, to begin with. He pounded the steering wheel and swore every time he had to stop for someone.

Eventually, we did arrive at the harbour. I was surprised to see the many docks. I knew the harbour area was the wealthiest neighborhood, but there were also several poorer areas near the docks and warehouses. On a point at the right, there was a tall, massive lighthouse, and to the left, there was a huge mansion on the cliffs just beyond the first long stretch of shops, cafes, and row houses.

There were many small, privately owned boats and yachts in the marina that bordered the main commercial street. The water was moving calmly, and the sound of it was soothing. The air was incredibly fresh, and the ocean was beautiful and enchanting. We walked out onto the pier, enjoying the view.

I heard some children's voices and turned. It was a family of five taking a stroll by the ocean. The sight of them brought more joy to my heart.

"It's so sweet," commented Cecilia, also looking at the family.

My eyes wandered beyond them as I noticed a large sign, which stated Ferry Café. So that's where it was. I would have to visit sometime.

"It's a wonderful place. We should go together soon," said Cecilia, who had followed my gaze.

I agreed, and we moved along, walking and

observing. Just around the bend, the sound of a violin could suddenly be heard, but it wasn't music, just the screeching of a bow on strings. In fact, the sound was almost painful. We came upon the man scratching away at the out-of-tune old fiddle right around the bend of the boardwalk. He had long hair, a hat for money in front of him, and seemed to be enjoying the awful sound he was producing. We both laughed at the fun of it.

Cecilia suggested we stop at a place called The Palm Cafe, which was situated on the long pier. It was a neat little yellow clapboard building. We chose outdoor seating and ordered fresh juice and boiled lobster with bread.

"The ocean is so calm today! It's soothing, don't you think?" asked Cecilia, smiling. She took off the pink cloche and shook her hair.

"Ah yes, I'm so glad to give my mind a break today. This is perfect."

"You've been working too hard?"

"I have to."

"Can you tell me more?"

"Well, I'm looking for a missing young woman. Her name is Aranxa."

"Oh, never heard such a name. I'm sorry."

"Well, her father paid me a very large sum of money. I'm trying my best."

"Well, that's the most important thing, to do your best."

In most cases, she would have been right — one's

best would be good enough. But in my case, failure to complete the task could mean something very dreadful for both me and Aranxa.

Once we'd finished the delicious meal, Cecilia said she had to go to an appointment shortly, and we headed to the main street to find another cab. Once I escorted Cecelia home, I decided to visit Mercedes and give her my updates.

The Hook Hotel couldn't be too far from the area of the harbour I had been in earlier. I asked around, and an old fisherman pointed me in the right direction. I happily walked along the water again, watching boatmen and fishermen go out into the waters or people going on with their business. Life was hard but also magnificent. Beautiful and horrible all at once. This thought brought a smile to my face as I soon reached The Hook.

As I entered this establishment, I was instantly met by a tall, weird-looking man with large eyes and giant hands. He pointed to the desk, saying nothing. I guessed he was mute. I told him I was there to meet a friend, giving him Mercedes' name, but this imbecile stood there for a good several minutes before pointing at one of the numbers on the wall behind him. Seventeen. That was the room number, I guessed. I thanked him through clenched teeth and went up the stairs to find the room.

The hotel itself was well-appointed and beautifully maintained, so I wondered why the owners would put someone like that at the front desk, even for short shifts. Perhaps he was a crazy son or something. I made a mental note to ask Mercedes about him.

I found the room and knocked while announcing myself. Shortly the door opened. There stood beautiful Mercedes wearing a short black dress. She smiled her impish smile.

"Very pleased to see you again, Mr. Nistage."

"And I to see you. By the way, it's just Luc, please."

"Sure. Come in, Luc, have a seat, and I'll get us a drink."

I sat down and noticed a phonograph standing on a corner table. Mercedes caught my look and went over to it, putting the needle to a jazz recording. I couldn't help but smile from ear to ear. I had always wanted one of those. Perhaps now that I had the money, I'd go out and buy one for my apartment here.

"So, Luc." She sat down and crossed her legs. I couldn't help but look for a moment but kept my focus on her pretty eyes right after. She placed our coffees on a small glass table between us. She was more beautiful than I remembered, and it took me aback. I had to make sure that in my mind, I always treated this as a business situation and nothing more. "What have you learned so far?" she asked, looking intently into my eyes.

I dived right into it, sparing no detail. It took a long time as she listened carefully, nodding and making notes. We had two refills of our coffee while I told her the story, and I felt completely alert, with my heart beating more intensely than usual.

"So, whom do you suspect the most as of right now? What do you think happened?" She asked the most difficult question once I finished my story.

I thought for a moment. "Well, I don't think this is a case of forced prostitution. I do have to investigate that possibility since I can't disregard anything yet. My gut feeling tells me it has something to do with the Sut Ni Tul clan."

"Well, that would mean this Mitch Stochild would be the main suspect if your information is correct."

"Perhaps. Maybe the scientist who's involved with him, Kramik—he's a smaller fish—could be a better one to follow first."

"Better, or easier? Will you check the other leads first?"

"Not sure if easier. Yes, I will try to speak to John Haster and Marie Toussant first and see what their reactions are."

A shadow crossed Mercedes' lovely face. "You must be very careful. These are powerful people."

"Oh yes, yes, of course. I'll make sure not to step over the limit with them, you know what I mean?"

Mercedes asked, "And what do you think about this Night Hawk? You really think he's only after members of the cult?"

"Eh...the murders have been brutal, but he's killed both men and women of all ages." I shook my head, puzzled. "It's hard to believe that all those people were cultists, but it could be true, too. In this town, nothing can be considered strange at this point."

"Okay, Luc, how about we meet again a week from today?"

"That's perfect."

I thanked Mercedes for her hospitality, and we shook hands. I left, planning to take the rest of the day off. I spent a lot of time relaxing on a bench on the pier, and when the sun began to set, I decided to enjoy a warm dinner at Heavenly Diner.

I elected to walk all the way back, and it got dark sooner than I expected. There were still plenty of people moving around, and I felt safe, but alas, not one day could go by for me without keeping away from hidden horrors. As I walked by one of the dark alleys, I saw what appeared to be a man quickly being pulled just around the corner of a building. He let out a short shout, but that was it. I stopped as if frozen. I had to make a decision.

I firmly gripped my revolver and took it out, looking around. There was no one who could have noticed either me or the other man, so I stepped into the dark alleyway. I moved as quickly as I could without making a sound, and as I got closer to the corner of a building, I heard something that sounded like an animal eating—beastly, slobbering sounds. I carefully looked around the corner.

What I saw next, no human can truly comprehend, or at least that's how I felt about it. There was a creature on the ground devouring the man it had grabbed. I had never seen anything like it. It had a dark red body, which was a disturbing mix of humanoid and octopus features. Long tentacles came from its back, and its prey was completely encircled by them.

It was horrifying. My throat closed, and my hand holding the pistol shook. The horror was beyond anything my mind could grasp.

I must have made a sound as the creature turned its head to face me. I shoved my fist into my mouth to keep from screaming. It had a large mouth with dozens of sharp, bloody teeth and huge, dead yellow eyes. It stared at me in silence.

I fired the pistol right at the beast's face.

The bullet hit the creature in the eye, and blood sprayed everywhere. The monster let out an insane ghastly howl and kept screaming and throwing itself against the wall. I turned and ran faster than ever before in my life to get out of there. Even blocks away, I could still hear it screaming. Windows and doors were opening, and people were looking in the direction of the unearthly sounds. I just kept running until I could no longer hear the screams. I figured the monster had either died or had survived and slunk away to hide in whatever hellish place it lived.

Finally, panting and exhausted, I stopped. Had that been the so-called Night Hawk?

I stayed the original course and finally got inside the Heavenly Diner. Sweating and with the terrifying sight still fresh in my mind, I sat down and stared at the white tabletop.

Bill hurried over to me. "You okay, Luc? You look like you've seen a ghost and been chased by the hounds of hell!"

All I could do was shake my head, my breathing still ragged and uneven.

Bill patted me on the back and said he would bring me some waffles and tea. I just nodded in agreement and closed my eyes.

I was still sitting like that when Bill set a cup of tea before me. I heard a phonograph begin to play a jazz record. Huh, Bill had gotten a phonograph too. Bill got himself a cup of tea and sat in the booth facing me. I sat back a little bit, keeping my hands on the table and focusing on calm breathing. As I raised the cup to sip, my hand was shaking like a leaf. I put the cup down and looked over at Bill, who was watching me with worried eyes.

The door of the diner opened. Jackson Thormund walked in, followed by four young men. That was the power of the Klan. The young were the easiest to brainwash with hatred and fear.

I hunched over the teacup and tried to be as quiet as possible, but of course, he noticed me. Thormund's eyes were narrow, and his gaze seemed angry, but he waved at me and then thankfully turned away and sat at a larger table with his group of young men. Bill got up to wait on them.

I went from seeing a beast monster to a human monster. But the human one didn't scare me all that much. Maybe he should have, for I had no idea how aggressive this man could get with his demands. I breathed deeply and raised my cup again. Now my hand was barely shaking. My mind was starting to clear the fog placed there by fear and sheer terror. Reason began to take over. I realized that there was no way the beast was the Night Hawk because Clara had told me that the Night Hawk left letters carved into his victims, and she'd said nothing about mutilated bodies.

Bill came up to me again.

"They are coming in late. Means they are up to something tonight, maybe something very, very bad," he said quietly and grimly.

"Hmm. Well, be careful, Bill."

"Yes, better play friendly with these wolves, or they'll think you're their enemy too. It's sad."

"Bill, what do you think of Night Hawk?"

"What's there to think about him? It's a demented, conniving man. The motivation of someone like that doesn't matter; he murders anyone and makes them suffer. I hope he is stopped soon."

"Ah, I suppose you're right. Do you think he's evil? Or insane?"

"Even the mad know when they go against God and continue committing evil deeds. It is someone bent on evil and refusing to ever change. The worst kind of person."

"Good point, Bill. What do you know of the Sut Ni Tul clan?"

"The cult of Sut Ni Tul. It's been around these

parts since even when I was a little boy. You can find some books written about the cults around here in the library archives. Back then, they lived in the woods, but now, I think there are many members here in town. It's impossible to tell how many."

"What is Sut Ni Tul?"

"I'm no expert, but I'm pretty sure it's a demonic creature from the depth of the ocean."

My blood chilled as I was overwhelmed by the mental image of the creature I had seen with my own two eyes. At this point, I was willing to consider anything.

"Is there a good Christian church around here?"

"Yes, Luc. I visit it. The best one is by the lighthouse. Father Brannahan tends to the lighthouse, but he is also the priest, takes care of the church. Very dedicated man. Loves Christ."

"Thank you, I will check it out. And can I have a refill?" I pointed at my teacup.

"Of course. And...prayer is powerful."

Bill went to get my tea, and I felt better after talking to him.

I pondered what it meant to be evil. Perhaps evil was, like Bill said, not an act at all, but choosing to persist in wrongdoing, making no effort to become better or to seek goodness.

I finished my second cup of tea and my meal, thanked Bill, left him a big tip, and sneaked out before Jackson could speak to me. I went quickly to my apartment, hastily locking the door behind me.

Sitting on the edge of my bed, I placed the good bottle of whiskey on the table next to me and quickly downed a glass, pouring a second one instantly. I knew this was the only way to get the horror out of my head and perhaps sleep, but of course there were no guarantees that terror wouldn't enter and torment my rest.

Suddenly a name came to my head, Gideon Slid. I took out my notebook and wrote it down, and placed it next to the bed. I was going to see the old professor tomorrow and see what he had to say about the Sut Ni Tul cult.

I drank more and more, making my head spin, but still, the terrible thing hovered at the edges of my mind. Finally, I must have passed out, for the next thing I knew, I was underwater, swimming among old black columns and buildings. They all had writing on them in a foreign language. In the distance, I heard a voice. It wasn't human, but I understood the meaning of the words.

"All of their memories...all of their memories... then make new...new memories."

I saw a forest of tentacles appear out of the water, then everything went dark.

CHAPTER SEVEN

I woke up with a terrible headache. Ugh. On the table, I saw the note saying "Gideon Slid" and remembered that I had decided to talk to him today, but first, I needed to clear my drumming head.

Stumbling, I went into the bathroom and threw cold water on my face. Then I went into the kitchen and drank two large glasses of milk. I prepared coffee and cut a piece of bread with butter, then I cut a nice thin slice of beef and once again sat by the window. It was later than I usually got up.

I slowly ate and saw a tall man in a black fedora show someone his badge. He was pointing towards the left side of the street and asking something. Then I saw him go right up to my apartment building and heard a knock on my door. I got up, and now walking more steadily, went to the door and opened it up.

"Yes, hello?"

The man at the door was just slightly older than I, and he had dark curly hair, blue eyes, and an aquiline nose. "I'm Detective Willems." He showed me his badge. "May I have your name, sir?"

"I'm Luc Nistage, private investigator, actually. I've been meaning to meet you. I have questions. Would you come in?"

He hesitated for a moment, giving me a penetrating look, but came in. We sat at my table. Unfortunately, one of my whiskey bottles was sitting there, but Willems simply gave me a wry look and smiled. I offered him coffee, and he smiled again and accepted.

"So, Luc, first my question. Did you see anything suspicious last night?"

I also laughed at this. If I told him what I'd seen, he'd send me straight to an asylum.

"Well, one of the things I won't mention because you'd think I'm crazy. The other is that I saw some Klan members in Heavenly Diner, rather late."

"Which clan...or cult?"

I paused and stared at him.

"Luc, if you're a good private detective, then you know already that in this city, nothing is too 'crazy' to mention and that we have more than one clan or cult."

"KKK."

"Jackson Thormund was there? There were two crimes committed here last night. A man was...torn to pieces. And another, a colored man, was beaten to death and hanged in one of the alleyways."

"Uhh...." My heart hurt as I looked over at the whiskey bottle.

"You should not be looking at alcohol to ease your stress. It'll only make it worse," said Willems. He was clearly a man of mental fortitude and focus.

I sighed and toyed with my coffee cup. "Yes, of course. But what if I told you...that I saw 'something' kill a man?"

"I'd believe you."

"Why?"

"I've seen a few 'somethings' myself in this city." Willems grimaced and drained his coffee cup.

"What do you attribute it to?" I was not yet ready to explain what I had seen or tell Willems that I had shot at the monster.

"Sut Ni Tul cult."

"And what are they? What does it mean?"

"You'd best talk to my friend." He took out a notebook and ripped off a sheet of paper, and wrote down a name and address. The name, ironically, was Gideon Slid. "What are you looking for specifically in this city, Luc?"

"I'm looking for a woman named Aranxa."

"Yes, I've seen her name on the list of those who have gone missing from the university." Willems leaned forward, focusing an intense stare on me. "Listen, we can help each other. You tell me what new information you learn, and in return, if I find out anything about her, I'll tell you. Also, would you be willing to testify against Jackson Thormund if we are able to get solid evidence?"

"Yes to both of those. What do you know of

Night Hawk? What letters does he carve into his victims? Does he kill members of Sut Ni Tul cult?"

"Not only them. This individual enjoys murder and carnage, and he's very elusive. The letters form words that make no sense, I'm afraid. I'll write them down for you." He did so on the piece of paper after checking his notes.

"So...and evil after all...."

"Would be evil even if it was only members of the cult he killed. One evil doesn't cancel out another. Evil is evil. Period. This is someone who's never considered the concept of mercy." Willems tucked his notebook into a pocket inside his coat.

"Yes, I understand," I replied. "I thought about this recently. Sin is part of us all. We all sin, but when someone continually destroys other lives... True evil is to crush another person's life, stealing from him the opportunity to break from sin, and have no guilt or shame in doing so. And then doing it again and again."

"That's about right." Willems stood. "It was good talking to you, but I must get to work again."

After Willems left, I felt a bit stronger. I had made another ally in this mad place.

Later that day, I stood in front of a brick row house with a grey door and blue window shutters. This was Gideon Slid's home. I knocked on the door and heard an old but strong voice from inside telling me to wait just a moment. I patiently waited until the door opened, and there stood a man with strong facial features, blue eyes, and short grey hair.

I smiled at this elegant gentleman. "Hello sir, my name is Luc, and I'm a private investigator. Detective Willems gave me your address after I spoke with him."

"Ah. If Robert turned you over to me, then I can probably guess the subject. Come on in."

I followed Slid. His was a very cozy home, with subdued lighting and heavy draperies covering the windows. He led me to a chair near a fireplace, which had a log burning. Then Slid sat down in the chair right across me and reached over to a small round table, picked up a pipe, and lit it. He sat there quietly, smoking for a while, looking at the fire.

"Tell me all you know," he finally spoke.

I told Gideon absolutely everything, including about the creature I saw in the alley. He sat there silently during my entire recital. The fire reflected in his eyes as he calmly puffed his pipe and watched the flames.

"The horror." He suddenly spoke in a calm, low voice. "It's been around for as long as we have existed. Long ago, many demons were able to take physical shape because of a breach in time's dimensions. This, perhaps, was caused by forces of evil or creatures from another place. Sut Ni Tul is one of those creatures. This monster feeds on people's memories. It sucks everything out of a person and makes his or her identity go away. The soul is still there but jailed inside a body that no longer functions properly, with a destroyed mind. The task of the clan is to create new personas out of those who are drained, make them new faces...

new names...."

I couldn't believe what I was hearing. "What do you mean, new faces?"

"It's literally what it means. With the help of the creature, the high priests of the clan developed skins...." Slid took in my astonished expression. "It's difficult to comprehend or to believe, I know." He paused and looked at me sadly, almost pityingly. "Know this, that in this town you must trust no one, and you must be ready to eliminate anyone. The only path for you to stay alive is the path of brutality and swift action and strong wit. You cannot fight Sut Ni Tul, but you can fight the humans he's commanding. I hope this girl you are looking for is still alive. And I wish you good luck and God's blessing."

Before I was about to leave, he tapped me on the shoulder.

"Do you dream? Because if you don't, if your mind is blank, that could be a sign you fell victim to the cult."

"Hah. I've had nightmares every night for many, many years. No problem with dreams."

He nodded and said his farewells.

As I stood outside of his house watching some people smoke, I felt that I needed my whiskey in hand. I knew that was a weakness. I indeed needed God's blessing, and I knew where I had to go next.

It was rather a rugged part of town, but it didn't feel dangerous. I saw homeless men sitting against walls of rundown buildings singing songs. Some sat by fires lit in steel drums in alleyways, and others tried to sell fish they had caught that morning. The way they looked at me held no envy or jealousy, and that was a surprise.

Up ahead was the point, a natural place for a lighthouse and a small white church. Perhaps that was the answer to why the poor were so calm in this area.

The wind was blowing more strongly today, and I had to hold on tight to my brown fedora. As I approached the small white wooden church, I noticed a tiny brick house right behind it with smoke coming out of its chimney. I walked up to the door, still battling the wild wind, and knocked. The door opened swiftly, and there stood a man with short black hair and a trimmed beard. He wore dark beige pants and a black shirt with a clerical collar. A thin string with a small wooden cross hanging from it was around his neck. His face was lined and kind.

"Father Brannahan?"

"That is correct, and you are?"

"I'm sorry. Luc Nistage, private investigator."

"Oh, well, do come in." He pointed to a simple wooden bench without a back support. He himself sat on a short wooden chair. The priest threw another piece of wood into the old fireplace. By the wall, there stood a flat wooden bed with an old mattress, one thin blanket, and no pillow. This was a very humble man.

"What can I do for you, Luc?"

"Well...I need help, Father." I paused and shook my head.

"There is no official language to address God, my son. Forget what you've been taught before. God knows your heart; he created your soul. You understand?"

I took a deep breath, and my eyes filled with tears. "I need...a blessing."

"Of course, a powerful thing indeed. You must connect with God to give you strength. Your faith has to be strong."

Brannahan stood up and opened a small wooden cabinet. Inside stood small glass bottles filled with different oils. He asked me to kneel and also took out a larger wooden cross and a metal cup. He put one of the oils on my head. Then he filled the cup with water and put it in front of me.

"Kiss the cross, son of God, and pray deeply with your eyes closed as I administer a blessing upon you."

I felt tremendous warmth going through my body as Brennahan placed his hands upon my head. The intensity of the warmth kept growing, and I felt a fire inside me, but there was no pain. It was a spiritual flame, giving me belief in myself as never before.

I hardly heard what the priest said, but he finished the blessing, and the heat gradually faded from my body. Would this blessing help me make the right decisions in a place as twisted and corrupt as this? I thanked Brannahan with all my heart as I left. He gave me a loving smile and said simply, "Just thank God." Then he gave me a small wooden cross on a string, just like his.

I hiked up to the cliffs and stood on the edge for a while, watching the waves crash against the rocks. The ancient ocean held so many mysteries in its depths, so much history, joy and suffering. It had been there long before I was born and would be there long after I was gone. The lighthouse stood as a beacon for those in danger, guiding them. How appropriate it was that a priest took care of it. The water mesmerized me as I stood still with my hat in my hands and the new cross around my neck. Was it strange that I had a pistol on my hip? Was it strange that even after this experience, I still knew that I possibly had to kill another human to survive this assignment? Was it strange that with the new peace I found came even more determination to do whatever I had to do? The waves smashed against the natural wall of the cliffs, the deadly dark rocks with sharp edges chiseled by a magnificent and powerful nature. For some reason, I knew that at one point, I'd be back at this very spot, looking out into the roaring ocean again.

That night I spent a long time in silence and the dark, sitting by my bed, thinking about my next steps.

CHAPTER EIGHT

The next day, around noon, as I was writing down my plans, there was a knock at the door. It was Cecilia. She invited me to the Ferry Cafe for a late dinner, and I accepted. In fact, I was excited.

Jazz, a festive atmosphere, and a beautiful woman to whom I was attracted made the recipe for a great time. However, I kept in mind where I was, and I was ready for more surprises the day might bring before my date, especially since I planned to sail to the island off the coast on my own.

It was around 1 p.m. when I made it to the harbour. I went to the marina and got a rowboat for rent without attracting any attention. The man who took my money was named Craighton. He was an old sailor, stern and rather rude, but he seemed to be straightforward and honest. He took my money and didn't ask any questions.

I also bought very good binoculars; I could actually see the island with them. I mapped out a circuitous route to diminish the chance of being seen if there indeed was anyone on the island.

I situated myself in the light but sturdy boat, checked the oars, and gave Craighton the signal. He pushed the boat away from the dock with his foot and spat to the side, looking disgusted. Wonderful fellow.

I began to row, and thankfully the waves were almost non-existent. I put all my strength into each movement. This wasn't going to be easy. A few seagulls flew over me, the sun was bright, but the temperatures were on the lower side. I felt a wind chill from the ocean breeze as I stopped rowing to give my body a break. I had filled my flask with water, so I had a few sips and used my binoculars to gauge the distance. To my pleasure, I saw a ship on the back right side of the island, well-hidden but still just visible to me. I decided to row towards the left side and picked up my pace.

The waves and the wind started to pick up, and I had to stow my hat under my leg so it wouldn't be blown away. Sweat began to drip into my eyes despite the chilly conditions. My muscles were getting fatigued, and this was a troubling sign, but nevertheless, I powered through the pain and reached the left side of the shore.

Jumping off, I had to wade into the water, and the chill shocked my senses for a moment. I pulled the boat well up onto the shore between some large bushes and trees and tied the rope around a tree. Then I sat down to focus on my breathing and to relax my body, and allow my muscles to rest a bit.

I slowly got up and began to move inland through the bushes and the trees, listening, but all I could hear was the twitter of little birds. One blue one sat on a tree limb, curiously twisting his head to the side to watch me.

As I went farther inland, there were fewer plants and more and more rocks. I was starting to climb higher as well.

I circled around a large group of boulders. I touched the stone formation with my hand, and it was very smooth. Then I thought I heard a sound coming from within the stones themselves, but I couldn't be sure because of the ocean waves and the birds. Suspecting that this was part of a cave, I took my bearings and quietly crept around until I found the opening.

I took a deep breath, gathered all my courage, and went in. A sandy path led downward, deep into the cave. I switched on my flashlight but doused it quickly as I approached a line of flaming torches along the cave wall. I could hear the sound of voices chanting. With revolver in hand, I went down the curving path.

Eventually, I approached a large open area and cautiously stayed hidden behind a rocky wall, for the area was filled with hooded figures, all in black, except for one man with blue eyes and blond hair whose robe was tied with white ropes. He was leading the strange chant. It was starting to hurt my head.

"Nug ga la ki ky

"Nit tu sul tak si

"Tuk yui opghuz

"Inrst goghz nahg!"

It was crazy, they were all repeating it after him, but suddenly silence fell. Two of them brought out a chair and placed it right in front of a dark opening in the wall. The blond man approached the chair. I heard screams coming from another corridor, and in a few minutes, they brought out a man who was struggling and fighting, but his hands were tied.

It was Charlie, the homeless harmonica player! The poor gent.

I broke out in a cold sweat as they sat him on the chair with his back to the opening and tied him firmly to it. They all began another, simpler chant.

"Sut Ni Tul

"Sut Ni Tul

"Sut Ni Tul!"

They kept going and going until an indescribable noise came from the darkness. Slowly two long, very thin tentacles appeared out of the opening in the cave wall, somewhat resembling an elephant's trunk at the end. The victim was screaming and shaking in horror as the tentacles wound around his head. There was complete and utter silence in the place except for Charlie's muffled screams, and a minute later, the man was silent. The tentacles uncoiled and drew back into the darkness. Charlie sat there with a blank stare on his face.

A large silver bowl and a plate with something thin on it were brought to the blond man. He poured some kind of liquid onto Charlie's head and then placed what looked like a thin white layer of something upon his face. Then some other minions covered the head with black cloth, and the leader opened a black book, and with one hand on Charlie, began to read from it. About five minutes later, he took off the cloth.

I was stunned and couldn't believe my eyes. Charlie had a brand-new face! This was the most terrifying thing I'd seen in this terrifying place.

The cultists untied him from the chair and helped him out of the room. Despite my shock, I knew it was time to move, and I swiftly made my way back out of the cave and down into the wooded area of the island. There I took a few deep breaths, still trying to comprehend what I had seen. Then, driven by my survival instincts (for my intellect was stunned), I rushed to my boat, dragged it into the sea, and began to row like a savage.

Oh, merciful God! Only You can guide me through this alive! All of my senses and humanity had been tested in this place, but I still kept going.

When I reached the marina, even Craighton's face registered shock when he saw the look of horror on my face. I didn't even thank him as I stumbled out of the boat to get a cab and make my way back to the apartment. I needed a drink of whiskey to calm myself before I went out with Cecilia.

As I rode back in the cab, my mind whirled. What a life! I'd experienced more intensity and madness in my short time in this town than in my entire life previously!

I sat in my apartment with my heart still pounding. I prayed and drank whiskey. Would Father Brannahan approve? I had to calm down. I remembered the words of Kasp Nudd, the war hero. Could he help me?

Maybe this was all just a dream, a long nightmare. But I looked in the mirror and could see that clearly, I was awake. I calmed myself and looked out the window at the setting sun. Nope, not a dream, but the strangest reality I'd ever experienced.

But it was time for my date with Cecelia. I put on my best suit and a fresh shirt and stepped out onto the street, looking around. My perspective had changed irrevocably — I couldn't help but wonder how many of the people walking around were part of the cult.

I refused to allow this paranoia to rule my evening. I knocked on Cecilia's door, and as it opened, she came out, looking joyful and ecstatic. It made me smile despite the fear that hovered at the edges of my consciousness.

We again took a cab to the harbour, and as I got closer to the water, the fear started to overtake me, and my heart began pounding hard against my chest again. Cecilia, who had no idea what dark turn my thoughts had taken, squeezed my hand as I smiled weakly at her. I hoped she attributed my subdued attitude to nervousness. I, however, was struggling to get the tentacles and the face changing out of my mind.

We entered the Ferry Cafe, and it was clear they knew Cecilia well. The maître d' put us at a table he referred to as her favorite.

The lights were dimmed, and we were brought some wine. I wasn't surprised that we were served illegal alcohol. Cecelia leaned close, a mischievous smile playing about her lips. "I know the owner well," she whispered. "He provides his regulars with special drinks." She lifted her wineglass in a salute to me and drank deeply.

Blue lights lit up the stage, and a man with medium-length black wavy hair emerged from behind the curtain. Three ladies followed and stood behind him. Cecilia said his name was Bryan. I raised a skeptical eyebrow, but the moment Bryan began to sing, I was instantly transported by the music, and I relaxed into my chair and absorbed the beauty of this pure and beautiful slow jazz.

"And the moon is so blue
And the river runs calm.
I am here with you
My love....
Oh darling, darling light,
I don't know why
My mind is always with you.
The night is so cool,
The wine warms my heart,
You are still here,
But I have to go soon...."

After the third song, I realized I had been so lost

in the music that I had nearly forgotten Cecelia. I drank some wine and leaned over to her. "I am so sorry; I did not mean to ignore you, but have been very absorbed by this music! He's a wonderful singer."

Cecelia laughed lightly. "I'm the same way." Then she entwined her arm with mine and laid her head against my shoulder as we listened to Bryan's mesmerizing voice. The wine indeed warmed my heart like in the song, and I was ready for the next one. Bryan sat on a stool to sing his next number. Each song had to do with some sort of romance or a broken heart.

> *"What must I do*
> *With such a perfect gift?*
> *In the morning of my life,*
> *I could stand by the tracks,*
> *Waiting on the train of time.*
> *But I chose to act.*
> *Oh this world*
> *That some find so dull!*
>
> *"Each moment with you,*
> *Is life come true.*
>
> *"There is despair*
> *For every lover.*
> *A heartfelt battle,*
> *But worth the struggle.*
> *Each moment with you,*
> *Is life come true."*

Cecilia waved at someone across the room. As I followed her gaze, all of my relaxation vanished as I saw, just a few tables away, the man with the blond hair and blue eyes from the cave, the Sut Ni Tul clan's high priest.

I managed to plaster a smile on my face as Cecelia grinned at him. "That's Mitch Stochild. He is a very important person in this city," she said. I nodded but did not intend to look in that direction again.

Bryan sang for another half hour, and I managed to calm down a little with more wine, but the feeling of an evil shadow hanging over me did not leave once I saw Mitch Stochild.

Cecilia and I took a cab back to our apartment house, and I was a bit unsteady on my feet from too much wine. We said goodnight at the doorstep. She smiled dazzlingly at me as she closed her door. I wanted to invite her into my place, but I held back.

It was the right thing, for once I lay in my bed, my mind went back to that cave, and I relived the horror I had experienced there. Finally, I fell asleep.

CHAPTER NINE

The following morning I headed to Heavenly Diner for breakfast. The server was a young woman. I asked where Bill was. "Dad has a cold," she said, and breezed away to put in my order. I was disappointed but didn't show it.

As I began to enjoy my first coffee and waffles, Jackson Thormund, whom I hadn't noticed earlier, pulled up a chair.

"Say, new guy, I got something for you."

I didn't want to hear what he had to say, but I feigned interest. "Oh yeah? What can I do for you?" I tried to keep my eyes on my plate and continue eating nonchalantly, but the waffles were like dust in my mouth.

"You're an investigator, right? I got a hundred dollars just itching to come from my pocket into yours for a small task."

"Okay, how small?"

"There is a guy, and we're suspicious of his

activities. A professor, seen plotting something with coloreds, name of Kramik. I never liked that guy, or his sponsor, that bastard Mitch. Anyway, listen—find out if it's true, okay? You just got to report to me one time backing up my agent's information, and the money is yours. He told me that late at night, he's seen them coming to his lab, brought in by some of his people."

I realized instantly that Kramik was most likely doing something horrible to those black folks, but this was a great opportunity for me to pit these two groups against each other and to find out exactly what Kramik was doing. So I agreed, and Jackson smacked me on the shoulder and looked very happy as he left the diner.

Nighttime was still far away, and I had plenty to do. First, I went to the police station to get John Haster and Marie Toussant's addresses and possibly to see Willems. I planned to speak with Kasp Nudd afterwards.

As I reached the station, I saw that it was a poorly-maintained old building with peeling dark blue paint. A wall plaque identified it as the oldest police station in the region.

As I stepped in and asked to see Robert Willems, a thin man with a giant nose stopped yelling at another cop and stepped up to me. "Who might you be?" he demanded, annoyed.

"Luc Nistage, private investigator. Is Detective Willems available?"

"No, he's out, but I'm Chief Sam Stoltz, and he answers to me. What do you need, new guy?"

"Oh, well, I need a couple of addresses so I can question a couple of people, namely John Haster and Marie Toussant."

To my surprise, Stoltz opened his mouth and roared with laughter. He grabbed his stomach and leaned back as if I had just told the best joke he'd ever heard.

"Oh boy, oh boy! Sure, sure!" he said, wiping tears from his eyes and continuing to chuckle. He grabbed a piece of paper and wrote down the addresses. His voice was filled with mirth. "You won't last too long here if you mess with these people, but that's great. I hate newcomers."

I thanked him calmly despite the inexplicably rude behavior and went on my way to John Haster's residence. It was an unexplored section of town for me, considered part of the harbour area, but actually not as close to the water. The house was a mansion set back from the road with on a large piece of property. In front stood a guard, a tall, bulky man with a full head of curly hair, smoking. I introduced myself, and he told me to wait, angrily grinding out his cigarette before going inside the house. He emerged again after a few minutes and told me to enter, head upstairs, and turn right.

I walked into the foyer. In front of me was a wide staircase with red carpet. As I strode toward the staircase, to the left, I could see a vast dining room with a fireplace, beautiful Victorian chairs and table, an Indian rug, and several paintings depicting beautiful women. I hurried up the stairs and turned right immediately. At the end of the corridor was a heavy brown door with two statues of nude women flanking it.

I knocked on the door and heard a firm voice welcoming me in. As I opened the door, I was surprised to see a rather small office. Behind a brown wooden table sat John Haster. He was leaning back in his chair in a relaxed posture, holding a book. Around the walls were shelves crammed with books. He gestured for me to sit across from him.

Haster laid aside his book and folded his hands on the desk. "I know who you are. I had a few men check you out. However, I have no idea why you would come to see me, so, please," he said, gesturing to me.

"I'm looking for a missing woman. Her name is Aranxa."

"Aranxa what?" he interrupted quickly.

"Von Dausen."

"Ah yes. The daughter of Allard. I know him from way back. He's not the type of man I'd, shall we say, mess with. You must be very good if he hired you," Haster said, regarding me through narrowed eyes. He hesitated for a moment as if taking my measure. "I will tell you, I've met this girl. And I'd bet you have heard rumors of what I do besides banking. But I'll tell you right now, even if I did want to mess with Allard, I'd never involve Miss Van Dausen. She's not the type that's good for business if you catch my drift. Not a particularly attractive young girl. So, I could just kick you out of here without giving you any information, but for some reason, I like you." Haster harrumphed. "I'm only going to say this once: I have nothing to do with her 'mystery.' Just don't go digging around in my parts of this town, or it won't matter how good you are, get it?"

Haster was shrewd, that was certain and very sure of himself. I decided that nonchalance was my best course of action. "Of course. But, uh, could you answer some other questions about this town?"

"Well, sure. You seem to be a respectful lad. What do you want to know?"

"Who owns the Ferry Jazz Cafe?"

Haster chuckled. "Ha. I do! You like it? Why do you wanna know?"

"Someone told me that she knew the owner."

"And who might that 'she' be?"

"Cecilia."

"Ah!" Haster smiled sardonically. "She's an angel, a very nice girl. Don't worry, I respect her too much to involve her in any funny business."

"Who do you think took Aranxa?"

The man's eyes narrowed, and I thought he might throw me out, but he answered, "Why do you think someone 'took' her? She could have run away! She could have drowned. She could have been a victim of Night Hawk, one of those whose heads he takes, you know? The possibilities are endless. Maybe she found a rich boyfriend and ran off with him. Is that what your senses tell you? That someone 'took' her?"

I maintained a cool calm. "Yes, that's what I think, and I feel she's still alive."

"Oh, and you say it with some confidence. Never failed a case, have you?"

"Depends what you mean by fail. I've always found the missing person. In a few cases, they were no longer alive, but those times I felt they were dead from the start."

"Oh, a natural God-given talent. Look at that, huh. Maybe I'll hire you sometime myself. Any more questions?"

"What can you tell me about Mitch Stochild?"

"Ah, Stochild. He's a very beloved figure in this town. Well respected, a gentleman. He sponsored the current mayor, and he owns several businesses. The public views him as someone who helps them and cares for them." John smirked while watching my eyes carefully. "Why do you ask? Is he a suspect?" His tone was mildly jeering.

"Everyone is a suspect."

"Except for me, remember?" Haster leaned forward.

I knew that if I said otherwise, it would not be a smart move. "Yes, except for you."

"Oh, lucky me! Why? Because I told you I'm innocent?"

"No, I just have a hunch."

"A hunch called fear." Haster laughed. "Well, anything else?"

"Last one. Do you know Marie Toussant well?"

"Yes indeed, we do business together. And sometimes, I am her client." He gave a sinister smile. "They also call her 'Madame Death.'"

"Who's 'they'?"

"The people who know her."

I decided to quit while I was ahead, so I stood to go. "Thank you for your time, Mr. Haster."

"I hope we don't speak again unless I have a reason to hire you. But that depends on how well you do in your current task."

I was happy to get out of there. Talking to him felt like being in the presence of a human reptile. He had a sinister aura, but as I had told him, for some reason, I really did feel that he had nothing to do with Aranxa's disappearance. He mentioned that he knew Marie Toussant well and was her client. For prostitutes or opium? Perhaps both, but he was a white slaver, besides being a banker. It was possible that he could have sold Aranxa, but then again, my gut said that was not what had happened. I pulled out my map of Paradise Harbour. I would have to give Mercedes an update to deliver to Allard, but first, I wanted to speak to Marie Toussant and visit Kasp Nudd.

As I neared the corner, there was a man shouting out headlines to sell newspapers. I purchased one, and straight away, on the front page, there it was in bold type, "Night Hawk Strikes Again!"

Why don't these powerful people put an end to this Night Hawk? I thought. Maybe they benefited from his killings. It kept attention away from the evils they were committing, even if they did lose some of their own. He was helping them, probably without realizing it.

There was no mention of KKK activity. This came as no surprise to me. On the inside, they had an announcement about a large event coming up at the harbour next week, with performers and sales booths, like a fair of some sort. They also had an article about a man creating an electric automatic traffic signal. General Motors was already interested in his patent. This man's name was Garret Morgan.

I put the newspaper inside my coat for further reading later and took a cab to Marie Toussant's building. It was an imposing row house with a water view in a safe and well-maintained neighborhood. The row of five houses curved around a garden with a fountain in the center, and she had the center house, the largest in the row. It was painted white with a red door.

I knocked, and a beautiful young woman in a skimpy, short dress and black stockings held up by frilly red garters opened up swiftly.

"Miss...Toussant?" I said, surprised.

The girl laughed. "No, I just work here. But Madame is home. Who may you be? I'll ask if she's expecting you, mister."

"Oh, she's not expecting me, but please tell her that Luc Nistage, private detective, is here to see her."

The girl closed the door, and after a few minutes, she opened it again and told me to go to the third floor and knock on the red door there.

As I made my way up the curving steps, I noticed that the walls were covered with art depicting women in varying states of undress. As I crossed the landing on the second floor, I caught a glimpse of a hallway with green doors. On each was a number. When I got to the third floor, there was only one door, the red one, which I knocked on. A smooth feminine voice welcomed me in.

As I entered, I instantly felt awkward and knew that the blood was rushing to my face. On a leather couch near a window with elaborate orange draperies lay an attractive woman in a short black dress, revealing her legs, also in black stockings with red lacy garters. She smoked a cigarette in a long holder. Her medium-length straight black hair was perfectly smooth, but her most startling feature was her large, bright green eyes, watching me with such intensity that I almost felt them pierce right through me.

"Sit, please. Luc? That's what Melia told me. So you are a private detective. That's very interesting."

As I sat down, she smiled and took out a small glass tube filled with white powder and a tiny delicate silver spoon. I knew the powder was cocaine. She put some on the spoon and motioned for me to snort it.

"Oh no, not for me, but thank you."

"If your answer is no, then this conversation will be a no as well. Only one time, for my pleasure?"

If she refused to talk to me, I would be cut off from one of the most powerful people in the town, someone who could possibly lead me to finding Aranxa. So I took the cocaine as she asked. It was unpleasant. I hoped that my senses were strong enough not to be disturbed too much.

"Well now, young, handsome detective, are you here to investigate me?" she purred as she waved her cigarette around.

"I'm looking for a missing woman. Named Aranxa Van Dausen."

"Van Dausen? Related to Allard Van Dausen?"

"His daughter."

"Oh, well!" She sat up, her dress exposing a great deal of her generous bosom. "What a tragedy for such a man to lose his daughter! He was my client a while back. I met him several times." She took the cigarette out of the holder and stubbed it out in an ashtray. "Frankly, very few things interest me in this town, and I don't pay attention to anything else."

I sat there for a minute, realizing that I'd used the cocaine for no reason whatever. I was irritated at the woman, but I stayed composed, unsure what more to ask at this point.

"What may those things be?"

She sighed, then said airily, "Money, young men, and drugs, Luc. What else is there?" She laughed as I sat there, regretting the question. I wrote down my information and handed it to her, asking her to let me know if she found out anything. Marie winked at me. "Perhaps if you do some favors for me sometime, there will be some information for you." Then she stood up gracefully, extending a slim, well-manicured hand out to me. Her skin was creamy and smooth, and I couldn't help but be attracted to her, but I thanked her for her time, and I was glad to go.

I walked, lost in thought, toward the canal, and sat on a bench. I pondered the situation for a long time. The sun was starting to set as I tried to gather my thoughts and align everything in my head. It occurred to me that darkness was not my friend in this place. Though I was close to Kasp Nudd's bookstore and The Dark Turtle, I felt weary and decided to go back to my apartment without visiting either establishment.

The sun was setting, and street lamps were coming on. I walked up the street, checking my map for the correct route home. Then several men in shabby clothes approached me, led by a bearded man in a nice black suit.

"Hey, asshole! I'm Ante Manland, and these are my streets!"

I didn't want to stick around and be shaken down or end up with some broken bones. I ran as fast as I could along the canal in the direction of The Dark Turtle, but I knew it was some distance away. The men chased me, shouting in anger. I was giving it all I had, lungs burning and feet pounding, when I realized they were no longer behind me. Here, the canal went under a building, and it was more or less a dead end. Breathing hard, I ducked into an alley, looking for a way back to where I'd been, when I heard a familiar, sickening chewing sound and quickly slunk behind a corner and into a dark opening in the wall. I sat there with my heart beating so loudly I was sure the creature could hear it. Fear flooded my body, and I held tightly to my revolver.

The creature was coming closer and closer. I could see one eye missing and blood from its latest victim dripping from its mouth. It could see me! It began moving toward me, the slavering mouth with its deadly, horrible teeth open wide. I froze in fear.

Then, bang! There was a gunshot. Blood splattered on the brick wall across from me as the monster fell dead, half its head shot away. Beside it stood Kasp Nudd, dressed entirely in black, holding a sawed-off shotgun.

"Not a good part of town to be loitering in the dark at night," he said to me.

I slowly stood up and faced him, my legs shaking.

"If you're gonna take on the Sut Ni Tul cult, Luc, you better get used to killing, and not just monsters like this one."

"Monsters...as in plural?" I croaked.

"Oh yes, there are a bunch of them. Not just this kind either."

"And what were you doing here walking around with a shotgun??"

Nudd shrugged. "I do that."

We mutely turned in the direction of The Dark Turtle and made our way there. I breathed deeply and slowly, trying to calm my racing heart.

As we entered The Dark Turtle and seated ourselves, it began to rain. Through the open windows, we could hear the drops on the wooden planks, roof, and the water in the canal. There were only a couple of other patrons in the bar, one a homeless man sitting in a far corner, drinking something warm. Maria approached, and I asked for a cup of black tea rather than a stiff drink. Kasp raised his eyebrows in surprise, but he asked for the same and told Maria to keep it coming. The owner, John, was behind the counter, talking to the same drunkard as last time, a man called Custard.

"So you have returned, as I said you would, Luc." Kasp looked out the window as the storm intensified. "This rain reminds me of a specific event during the war," Kasp said quietly, a faraway look in his eyes. "It was pouring just like this, and I had been sent to steal some documents from a small enemy base. Because of the rain, I was able to sneak up behind each guard and eliminate him one by one. Then I went inside — can you believe it was unlocked? — and took the documents while everyone else was asleep. After that, I set the whole place on fire. Fire and rain, dancing together. It was incredible." Kasp shook his head, smiling slightly at the memory, and sipped his tea.

"Well, let's keep the fire out of the equation this time," I said, forcing a smile. It was disconcerting hearing how casually Kasp spoke about killing people.

"This is good tea, shocking for a dump like this. Hey, John!"

John turned to Kasp and indicated he was listening.

"Is this a British tea brand?"

"Yorkshire, yes."

Nudd nodded in satisfaction. "Ah, yes, yes. I had this a few times during the war. I'll find out later where he got it. I want some for home."

"You live near here?"

Kasp nodded again. "That bookstore is also my home. I live 'above the store,' as it were."

We sat quietly, drinking our tea for a moment.

Finally, I spoke. "Kasp, what do you propose we do?"

He looked at me penetratingly. "I like how you think. You ask direct questions, the hallmark of an honest man. You have very respectable qualities. Frankly, our task is quite simple. We find out more about the cult and eliminate its leaders. But it is important that we have concrete, immutable proof of their crimes."

I swallowed hard. "I have concrete proof. I know who the leader is and the scientist who is working for him. I saw something with my own eyes."

Kasp smiled mysteriously and leaned forward. I told him everything I knew. He listened carefully.

"We can check out Kramik's lab tonight. If those reports by Thormund are accurate, we could get lucky," said Kasp, finishing his third cup of tea.

"In the rain?"

"The storm's passing now. And besides, the

sound is good cover for our movements."

We paid John and bid him goodbye and spent the next hour making our way to the university lab on foot. We hid behind a wall, looking for signs of activity inside. After about twenty minutes, I was starting to get anxious, but Kasp Nudd looked as relaxed and calm as he had the entire night. I stretched out my legs and put my head against the cold wall. My clothes were wet, and I was feeling quite fatigued. Another hour passed.

"There we go!" whispered Kasp, finally.

Two cars drove up to the doors. Out of the first came Kramik and a tall man with a gun. Two men in identical outfits emerged from the second car, and with them were two sorry-looking fellows, one colored and the other white. Kramik and his henchmen took the two men inside the lab. Kramik was laughing and joking with them.

"Let them all settle in, then we go."

"How about the two men?"

Kasp's face was furious. "Don't shatter my assessment of your intelligence, Luc!" he hissed. "Do you want to take their place on the operating table? Or perhaps learn nothing? I am an expert in combat, in espionage, in stealth. Okay?"

"Yes, I'm sorry."

"Now, focus, my friend." He slapped my shoulder.

We sat there for another twenty minutes, Kasp alert as a fox on the hunt. He made the sign to move, and we silently ran up to the door. Kasp used a tiny metal pick to unlock it. He eased it open just a crack and peered in with one eye. Then Kasp jerked his head at me to follow, and we slipped through and eased the door closed.

We hid behind a nearby desk, watching a guard at the other end of the hallway. He seemed distracted and bored, looking out a window.

As I sat waiting for Kasp's next move, I wondered if my body had any adrenaline left and if any of these crazy actions would help me find Aranxa. My gut told me they would, but I sure couldn't see any connections yet.

Kasp squeezed my shoulder when he noticed my thoughts were far away, and I snapped back to reality.

We crept quietly down the hallway. Kasp held a large bolt in his hand, eyeing a mirror a few yards away. Suddenly he flung the bolt against the mirror, shattering it, and the guard ran past, not seeing us. In a flash, Kasp was on him and stabbed him in the back and laid him out on the floor without making a sound.

Swiftly and silently, Kasp and I moved down the hallway, up the stairs, and crawled, staying in the shadows, into a large room. It featured a twisting metal stairwell going further up. In a chair next to it was another guard, fast asleep and snoring. Another guard stood outside an open door on a balcony, keeping watch over the grounds outside. Kasp did not take long to eliminate these men as well, and we made our way up the spiral stairs.

There behind a glass door, we saw the lab. Kramik was focused on his work. To my absolute horror, I could see two bodies on separate tables, already dead, with their faces stripped of the skin and other parts of the bodies missing skin as well. Kramik was busy mixing some kind of potion.

Kasp nodded at me, and we burst into the room.

"What the hell are you two doing here? Guards!" Kramik yelled.

Kasp laughed and stepped closer to him. "Your guards are taking a nap until their next reincarnation."

"You bastard! And you're that pathetic private investigator! You little snake, you'll get nothing from me."

Kramik moved to grab a gun, which was hidden underneath the apron of his work table, but Kasp was faster and punched him in the stomach and then stabbed him in the same spot.

What followed next was as nearly as horrific as Kramik's work. Kasp lodged his thumbs into Kramik's eyes and crushed them, blood spurting. Kasp laughed like a psychopath and then broke Kramik's neck.

I stood there in shock.

Kasp grabbed a towel and began to clean the blood from his hands. "Well, that was a bit exciting! I'm going outside to be on the lookout; you look for what you need to find here and get out soon."

He was as calm as ever, enjoying the casual carnage and brutality. The man who was now my partner was also a demented individual.

Kasp went down the spiral staircase. I shook my head hard, slapped myself, and turned on the tap to throw cold water on my face. Then I took a closer look at what Kramik had been doing.

He had carefully cut the facial skin away and laid it in a flat-bottomed basin. I realized that during the cave ritual, facial skin was what they had put on Charlie. But how had they held it in place? How did it adhere to the victim to completely alter his looks? I had no idea what else happened during the dark ritual. Maybe the creature's tentacles did something I couldn't fathom.

I wondered what would happen if one of the changed people died. I left the lab and examined the bodies of the guards, pushing and pulling their facial skin. I could not tell whether they were normal or people who had undergone the face change. Well, now I knew more about what they did, even if I was not sure how they did it. I forced to the back of my mind the knowledge that I had partnered with an insane maniac.

Kasp Nudd first took me to his bookstore, where we got cleaned up. He gave me a fresh shirt after I got most of the blood off my coat. He drove me home himself, for I was completely exhausted and couldn't handle another adversary that night.

I fell asleep surprisingly quickly despite all the terror I'd witnessed.

In my nightmare, I was walking through the streets of Paradise Harbour, and there were dead bodies all around, and at every corner, someone was crying in sorrow. I could see a green light coming from the ocean. As I got closer to the water, it illuminated the sky and the waves. Then out of the ocean came long, thin tentacles, dozens of them. They stretched up high and danced in the green light. I was horrified, but I could not move. I wanted to wake up but couldn't do that either.

Suddenly everything went dark, and the next thing I knew, I was in a rowboat on the canal, relaxing. The sun was shining brightly, and the birds were singing. It was no longer a nightmare!

I woke up, but for the first time in years, I didn't want to.

I took a deep breath and smiled, feeling relaxed and happy, but then the memories of the previous night rushed in, clouding my mind like a dark mist. I was back in reality.

Chapter Ten

That night Cecilia and I went to the Ferry Cafe for the second time. We were anticipating the performance of the red-haired woman from the advertising poster. Her voice was smooth and beautiful, and she gracefully moved around the small stage. All the attention was on her.

"And the oceans have parted
For me and you,
Like a heavenly guidance
Just for us two.

"I see I was dreaming,
It was a beautiful dream,

"But now you are leaving.
I thought it was forever.
Why are you going?
My body can't shake the fever.

"Is this a disease
Whose name is loneliness?
Forgetfulness
Who am I?
Who am I?"

The sad songs she sang constantly reminded me of the secrets I knew about Paradise Harbour and my own nightmares. The singer's soothing voice and alluring movements, along with the lulling sounds of the instruments, did nothing to calm my mind.

Things only got worse after the performance was over. As we rose to leave, Mitch Stochild approached us. He introduced himself to me with a big smile. I managed to treat him cordially.

"You two look lovely together, and you obviously love the jazz here. Isn't it amazing?" He turned to me. "And what do you do, Luc?"

"I'm a private investigator, and I love the jazz here; it's absolutely wonderful."

"Well, you certainly have come to the right town to ply your trade. Have you heard of the Night Hawk?"

"Yes, it's, uh...very disturbing." I understood why animals had a fight-or-flight instinct.

"Yes, and I recently got news about a friend of mine falling victim to this savage killer." Mitch shook his head. "Hey, we should cheer up. There are a lot of wonderful things out there. Humans are the greatest creation in the universe." Mitch proceeded to order a few drinks. "Sit down, sit down. We play by our own rules in this café, as you noticed," he added.

"It seems that a lot of this town plays by its own rules," I observed.

Mitch was unperturbed. "That's what makes our town so special. A great mix of people and beliefs, all together. It's a new age, true progress. We don't discriminate...well, at least most of us here don't."

"The Night Hawk doesn't either, I suppose."

A scowl fleetingly crossed Mitch's face, but he quickly turned all smiles and said he had to leave. "I hope we can talk sometime," he said to me as he made a slight bow in Cecelia's direction. She beamed at him.

That night I still did not ask Cecilia to come inside. Even though she had nothing to do with my investigation and it wasn't immoral or illegal, I felt I shouldn't.

I ended up going to Bill's diner after parting ways with her. I sat down and ordered coffee. Then Jackson Thormund stormed in as if he had been watching for me. He approached quickly, his eyes shining as he pushed three hundred dollars into my hands.

"You really outdid yourself! I sure underestimated you!" he chortled. "Those bastards! You really did a number on them. I got an early look at the newspaper story. I love that touch with that moron's eyes...hahaha. Ahhh, well enjoy your coffee, brother, enjoy!"

He jumped up and left after that astonishing speech.

I sat there realizing that now I could possibly gain the reputation of being strongly associated with the KKK, and this could bring me under suspicion by Willems. I suppose it was a good thing I had approached Haster and Marie since they had the police department under their control, and I could guess that they didn't mind Thormund. Surely they had dealings with him. I puzzled over Aranxa's notes. I realized she had mentioned other people from the university, especially Doctor Ambigo, as a good friend. I had to speak with him. She also mentioned meeting Father Brannahan and a priest named Smith, feeling down and afraid and getting a blessing and visiting the church a few times, as well as feeding the poor. I had to go back to the church and talk to both of those men.

Bill came back to my table as I was lost in thought. "Well, some friend you made."

"He's not my friend."

"Well, he sure thinks so! But don't worry, Luc."

"Impossible not to worry."

"More tea?"

"Yes, please."

My stomach growled, and I recognized I needed food, not just coffee. I ordered some rye bread with butter and cheese and eggs.

The last few patrons left the diner, and I was the only person sitting in the eatery. I watched the street outside. It was, as usual, dimly lit and deserted.

Occasionally I saw a cat, but as I focused on the street, I could just make out a man in a white coat standing against a wall, with a hat pulled low over his face, and I knew he was watching me. Bill brought my food, and I turned to thank him. When I looked out the window again, no one was there. Were my eyes playing tricks on me? No. I was certain he was the same man I had seen on the train. What did it mean? Who was he?

I let out a long breath. The "one day at a time" philosophy was difficult to live by in my situation—I had to think and calculate. I was investigating very dangerous people and was putting myself in the sights of deadly individuals.

"You've been having a rough night?" asked Bill as he took my plates.

"I suppose. But that's just how it is."

"My wife is sick—I've been having a tough time too. My mind just can't be at ease." He shook his head sadly.

"I'm sorry, Bill. I hope she gets better soon."

"Well, hope dies last, does it not?"

Back at my apartment, I found a new note from Mercedes summoning me for an update. She also noted that Allard was coming into the city with more men, and she assured me that he still had faith in me and that I was the prime investigator in the case.

This night I once again dreamed of an underwater city inhabited by horrific creatures.

In the morning, I decided to leave very early and walk to see Mercedes.

As I was walking through the streets, which weren't quite awake yet, I heard the sound of a harmonica playing and saw a man standing with his back to me. Charlie? It couldn't be, not after what I had witnessed on the island. It was a different type of tune from those Charlie used to play, and I circled around and looked at the man. It was indeed the new face I had seen on the island. The man looked perfectly normal — there was no way to tell this was not his original visage. I approached him, and he smiled.

"Hello, Charlie."

The man stopped playing. "I'm sorry, sir, you must be confused. My name is Tom."

As I stood there in silence, something deep inside me woke up, something primal. A deep rage boiled up in me, rage against the cult and also toward this man, although it wasn't his fault; he was a victim.

My judgment was clouded. Perhaps the things I'd witnessed were turning me toward violence to solve these riddles. Still, I asked the man to come with me, saying I'd pay him well for a little private concert. He followed me into an alley lined with abandoned buildings. I took him into a small backyard with brick walls and indicated that he could stand against a wall and play for me. He did as I asked, looking a little confused, and as he lifted the harmonica to his lips, I took out my revolver and shot the man twice in the chest.

There was an incredulous look in his eyes as he collapsed. I felt my rage calming as I watched the life fade from his body. Then the face seemed to go soft and almost melt. I knew what would happen. I dreaded doing it, but I pulled at the skin on the face, and it came off in my hand. There lay Charlie, dead. Murdered by me, or by both the cult and me.

So the face and the ritual were meant to stay only on the living. But how this information was worth this man's life, even if it was a fake life, escaped me now that my insane rage had subsided. I felt tears well in my eyes as I looked at Charlie one more time and said a quick prayer, then I ran out of there before anyone could find me next to the body.

I sat on a bench just a few blocks away from The Hook Hotel and watched as the town came alive in the bright cool morning. I wanted to be as calm as possible before updating Mercedes, and I had to keep the information about what I had just done hidden.

When Mercedes welcomed me in, looking as beautiful as ever and wearing an elegant red dress, I immediately heard music and remembered that I was going to buy a phonograph myself. I took out my notebook and wrote a reminder. I had too much on my mind to remember such things.

We once again sat across from each other, and I told her what I had learned, leaving out certain things that I deemed could spell trouble for me, such as what I had done with Kasp and to Charlie. She was shocked about the cult leader's abilities and the creature.

"How do you know about the new facial features being 'conditioned' to the person's life energy?" she asked, puzzlement creasing her lovely brow.

"I discussed it with an expert in this matter," I answered, lying through my teeth.

She seemed satisfied with this and went on to tell me when Allard Van Dausen would arrive and that I would be meeting with him in person.

I left, nervous about my impending meeting with Dausen. I needed to increase the pace of my work even more. I made my way toward the church to speak with the priests. Then I'd have to find Dr. Ambigo and talk to him.

As I neared the church, Father Brannahan and another priest were talking to some homeless folks right on the street as they set up some tables. Father Brannahan smiled and greeted me when he saw me approaching. "Luc, very nice to see you again. How have you been feeling?"

"Is there a more private spot we can talk?"

He showed me into a small abandoned home, and there we sat on two old wooden chairs. The place was terribly dusty. I had not noticed during our previous meeting how worn and wrinkled the hands of Father Brannahan were. This man did not just act like a saint but worked like one as well.

"What worries you? The Lord is always ready to aid you."

"Father...the woman I'm looking for, Aranxa, she received a blessing from you as well. Do you remember anything about her?"

The priest's face showed concern. "Oh yes,

poor thing, she was not in a good state. She was very depressed, sad, spoke of horrible, unbelievable things. Her mind was affected by Satan. It was sad. I did my best, but she never returned."

"Can you be more specific?"

"She said that people who were monsters were after her and that there were people who were not real people. I didn't understand her too well, but I let the Lord do the work. Whatever happened was her life path." He shook his head.

"Father, you meet a lot of people who are existing at the margins of society. Have you ever heard things like this before?"

A sad, faraway look came into the priest's eyes. "The mental illness that afflicted Aranxa has afflicted others here from time to time." He shook his head. "I try to help these people, but most of them are itinerants. They leave, and I never see them again."

I sat in silence for a moment. So was it the cult after all? Mitch Stochild? That would explain why Father Brannahan's acquaintances "disappeared." Or maybe they were itinerants. What had Aranxa found out, and how? How could I learn more? Would I have to become Stochild's friend or spy on him every night?

I thanked the kind priest and went on my way to the university, but I wasn't sure if I could do much by gleaning information from outside the cult. I would have to get inside. The idea sickened and frightened me.

My mind was racing as I went through various

scenarios in my head. Logic told me that Aranxa was no longer alive, but my gut feeling didn't agree, and I felt I was close. Never before had my intuition let me down, but this case was special.

I reached the university during a class change. Many students were walking in and out, police were there questioning people, and there were more security guards than usual.

Of course! The newspaper had announced what had happened to Kramik! I hoped this would not interfere with me finding Ambigo quickly. I entered the hall and saw Sara at the desk again. She looked extremely tired, slumping at her desk and sporting large circles under her eyes.

"Hi, Sara. I don't want to bother you much, but could you please direct me towards Doctor Ambigo's office?"

She wrote something on a piece of paper. "I'm not supposed to do this, but he hasn't been in for a while, and some are very worried." She glanced up at me meaningfully. "You know...ah...what happened here...so this is his address."

"Thank you very much. I'll go there immediately." I left with a feeling of foreboding. I managed to find a cab since Ambigo's home was a part of the town I hadn't yet explored, and time was of the essence.

The cab stopped about six blocks away from where I had it marked on my map, and I looked at the young driver with a question in my eyes.

"Ah, sorry, mister, you're not from around here. This part of town was flooded, and it hasn't recovered since it's lower than the rest of the city and close to the water. The streets are mostly flooded here, with the exception of a few spots that are unreachable by car. Everyone who still lives here uses either the boardwalks they built along most of the buildings or boats."

Well, that was surprising. I thanked the driver and paid him.

I walked a bit further and saw what he was talking about. Indeed, all the streets ahead looked like small canals. I found where the wooden boardwalk began. It was creaky and poorly put together, probably in a hurry, and undoubtedly most of the rich in this city did not care to help, nor did the politicians owned by those very people. I picked my way carefully, expecting the boards to break any moment.

As I continued along this narrow, strange path, the scenery changed. There were many more red brick row houses, and often I saw signs for theaters or gentlemen's clubs, which all seemed to be closed down.

I finally saw another person. He was sitting on a bridge connecting two blocks, wearing old tattered clothes and fishing. He seemed young, but his face was rough, most likely because of life circumstances.

"Are there a lot of fish here?"

He slowly turned his head toward me and stared at me silently. The longer this went on, the more awkward I felt. His sad eyes seemed empty of meaning, and he seemed to search for a reason to speak but then chose not to as he turned his gaze back to the dark waters below.

I was unsurprised. I continued on the path, but then I came to a place where it had broken. There was a small rowboat attached to the end of the structure, with a very long rope connecting to the other side, so it could go back and forth if pulled. There were two oars inside. I slowly and carefully got in. As I began to row, I heard something splash in the water nearby. I felt goosebumps crawl on my skin, a bad feeling.

I looked back, and the bridge was a bit far away now, and the man was still there in the same position. Suddenly something pushed the boat from underneath, and it rocked violently as I saw something break the surface of the water, but then it was gone again. I continued to row, but now in a frantic fashion as my heart raced. I jumped onto the boardwalk as quickly as I could once I reached the other side. I pulled my revolver and watched the water but saw nothing moving. I kept my revolver in my hand as I continued my walk. I saw the sign for Striker Street, and I double-checked the address. I turned to my right and found the row house with the number I was looking for.

The door was slightly open. My heart beat faster again, and a feeling of dread flooded me. This was never a good sign. I knocked several times anyway and waited. There was no answer. I opened the door and called out for Dr. Ambigo. Nothing.

I entered the house and flipped the light switch. The lights did not work, although there was enough daylight coming through the windows to see well. As I entered the main room, I saw a trail of blood leading into a small office room on the right side. I took a deep breath and blew all the air out, and then entered the office.

In the center of the room lay the man I had seen arguing with Kramik on one of my first days in the city. I bent down to examine the body.

Ambigo had a curved knife stuck in his chest, and his eyes were missing. As I got closer and examined the knife, I saw that it had engraved images of tentacles on it. The cult had killed Ambigo, and they hated him so much that they hadn't even put any effort into changing him. Or, perhaps with Kramik being dead, they had tried to make Ambigo do the scientific parts of their evil deeds, and he had refused. That had to be it. If he was a brave man with honor and convictions — I remembered that he'd been polite to me even when angry — that was surely it. Sometimes this was how the good ones ended up. I shook my head, covered the body with a throw that was draped on the sofa, and searched the house.

I riffled through all the papers in the office, searching for any mention of Aranxa. I yanked open all the desk drawers and felt all around them. I was rewarded when I located a small notebook tucked inside a tiny shelf built under the center drawer. Written on the front was the word "Faces." I tucked it inside my coat and left.

It was just as nerve-wracking coming back out of the neighborhood as it had been going in, but I managed to stay in one piece. Once outside, I had to walk for a long time before I saw any cars or cabs. As I stepped into the street to hail one, a car stopped next to me. In it sat Mitch Stochild.

"Luc! Lovely to see you like this. Please come and sit. Join me for an early dinner. My chefs are making their seafood specials today!"

That had to be one of the last things I wanted to do. "Oh well, I—"

"No, no, no, don't get humble on me. Come on, get in. I'd love to have your company. You will enjoy this food, I guarantee it."

I got into the car with Mitch and his chauffeur, whose face looked distinctly fishlike, and we moved on.

"Yes, Luc, Mike is an ugly one...hideous."

"Oh, no, I—"

"He's deaf. He won't hear us. He can read lips, but not while his eyes are on the road." Stochild laughed mirthlessly. "So, what were you doing in this part of town?"

"Part of my investigation."

Stochild frowned thoughtfully. Was this an act? "I'm sorry, I heard a bit about your investigation from either you or someone else, but I don't recall what you are looking for. Can you remind me?"

"I'm trying to locate a missing woman."

"Ah, that's rough in this city. Well, we are almost there."

The car passed through an imposing pair of gates and went up a hill, where stood a mansion overlooking the ocean. We got out, and I admired the spectacular view. Mitch smiled and waved for me to follow him into the enormous house.

It had heavy white Corinthian columns at the front and large green double doors. The handles of the doors were metal and together made the shape of an octopus. My eye twitched as I did my best to show no reaction and smiled at Mitch.

It was even more amazing and impressive inside. The ceiling was very tall, with a large, beautiful crystal chandelier lighting the generous entry. I looked at the mural painted on the ceiling. It was a depiction of a giant squid taking down a ship during a storm in the ocean, and on the cliffs nearby was a house similar to this one.

"You like the art?" asked Mitch.

"Oh, yes, very...interesting...original."

"I love the sea, with its mysteries. It is ancient, timeless."

"God's wonderful creation."

Mitch did not reply to that comment, as it seemed to bother him. From my point of view, he was a demon worshiper, so it made sense that the mention of God did not bring him any joy.

He invited me into the next room. The fireplace in it was lit, and beautifully upholstered red chairs and a table were close by. "Not the traditional dining spot, but I prefer this room for my meals. I hope you don't mind?"

"Of course not. This room is also stunning."

In the corner of the room stood a statue of a woman with two tentacles instead of arms. On the wall near me hung a large portrait of a man in a grey suit with a clean-shaven face and a very serious expression.

"My father never did learn to smile," Mitch laughed, and as he did, the servant, who was referred to as Sid, brought us wine, water, and some rolls with sliced cheese on the side. Mitch gestured for me to sit. "Enjoy our little appetizers before the seafood, Mr. Nistage."

I almost asked if I could bless the food to test his nerves but chose not to. After all, I needed to get close to him.

I tried the rolls, and the bread was soft and homemade, and with sweet butter melting on top, they were the most delicious rolls I had ever tasted. I took a bite of the cheese, and it was equally delicious. The wine was slightly sweet and also of very high quality.

"I see by your expression that you are enjoying the food already." Mitch smiled at me as he downed the wine in his glass.

"Yes, it's amazing."

It was hard not to be distracted by the excellent food, and I had to remind myself whose company I was in and why.

"My chef, Christopher, is a master. I found him

in England, working at a port restaurant. He was the best find during my travels around Europe."

"I'm glad you have invited me to experience it."

Mitch sat back in his chair and popped a square of cheese into his mouth. "So, Luc," he said, swallowing. "How long have you been doing investigative work?"

"Just a few years, actually." I sipped more wine and felt the warmth of the fire. I was less tense now.

"But in just a few years, you've managed to do well, I assume? I heard your client is Allard Van Dausen."

I shrugged, acting nonchalant. "Perhaps I'm just fortunate. I did well in some missing persons cases, with quick results."

"And how have your results here been so far?"

"I'm making some breakthroughs." Sid filled our wine glasses again.

Mitch smiled. It looked genuine. "I hope you find who you are searching for. Life is very mysterious. If you search for something with all your energy, sometimes it finds you or is drawn to you." Was it my imagination, or was there a warning in his words?

"I hope you're right."

"I am right, but the result is not always good."

Chills ran down my spine, and I struggled to keep my expression neutral.

Stochild was such a charismatic man. It made sense that he could lead this cult. Brainwashing required an individual to seem inspirational, charismatic, and even kind.

Now Sid removed our dishes, and another servant appeared with new dishes filled with seafood. Shrimp, fish, crab, and calamari — octopus. Mitch grinned widely.

I tried the shrimp and fish first and wasn't disappointed. Chef Christopher was indeed a genius. I avoided the octopus but ate the crab next, and the meat melted in my mouth.

"Luc, in your line of work, danger is a big factor. How do you deal with fear?" Mitch looked at me quizzically.

Again, I tried for nonchalance. "I allow it in. If I repress it too much, then in a critical situation, it can paralyze me. But experiencing it often and knowing it well, I feel more capable when things get rough."

"Hmm, that's an interesting view." He cracked a crab claw with a small device made for eating seafood and used a pick to pull out the meat. "Of course, people who have mental issues feel no sense of fear at all. Just a sense of brutality. They lack other emotions as well. No pity for others, for instance. Don't you think this Night Hawk is such a person?"

I nodded. "I think you're right that he's an intelligent madman."

"Intelligent...or simply a force of nature. The identity of the Night Hawk may not be such a secret to some in this city, but perhaps... Eh...never mind. Are you enjoying your meal?"

"It's the best I've had. Can't remember ever eating better seafood than this."

"Good. You are an interesting man, Luc. Genuine, not corrupt."

He was praising me, and I had to stay on guard. Mitch was possibly my biggest nemesis in this city and clearly a very dangerous person, and I certainly did not want to be his friend.

"What do you think evil is, Luc?" he asked suddenly.

I chose my words carefully. "Evil is to do terrible harm to another person and to keep repeating these acts without an effort to improve."

Mitch inclined his head. "And what if these acts improve society?"

"For me, nothing can trump individual liberty and life."

"Ah...like the Founding Fathers. You are a man of strong principles. We both would make good generals, with very different views, though. Well, Luc, I must attend to business now," he said, placing his napkin on the table. "But thank you for the company. My driver shall take you to your home now."

I thanked him and left the mansion with the deaf driver.

That night Cecelia and I met at the Ferry Café. There were two performers: Phillipa, an attractive French woman in her thirties with a soft, low voice, and Leonora, a young American woman with big black eyes and curly black hair, her voice as rich as a cup of coffee laced with brandy. Together they sang a smooth and silky duet, which put the whole audience at ease and created a peaceful and relaxing atmosphere, almost enchanting. Everyone was drinking, sitting back, and dreaming with their eyes open.

"She came to the ocean,
The waves were so high.
The light of the lighthouse
Signaled, 'It's time.'

She felt all alone
With the big world revolving.
She put on a mask
To hide all the hurting,

'You must come with me,'
Whispered the prince of the sea.
'Why not come with me?'
Asked the voice from the deep.

She then felt a prompting,
An unstinting urge.
Her mask was made solid.
None could tell it was forged.

She lay by the dark water
And smiled at the prince
Within the deep ocean
Great powers agreed.

'You must come with me,'

Whispered the prince of the sea,
'Why not come with me?'
Asked the voice from the deep

She stood by the lighthouse,
And knew all was false.
She tore up the mask,
And took a deep breath.

The light in the distance
Told her to have faith,
And the strongest of all things,
To feel the Lord's grace."

I paid close attention to the lyrics, unlike most of the other patrons. These two ladies were telling tales of something or someone close to their hearts, and there was more to these words than fiction and fantasy. I looked over at Cecilia and was surprised to see her eyes filled with tears. Perhaps something inside of her was moved by this song — a beautiful song, indeed.

I saw Mitch there, but he greeted us briefly and left swiftly. As Cecelia and I walked outside, hand in hand, I made up my mind to invite her in tonight, but again, it was not meant to be.

As we got strolled nearer our street late that night, we heard horrible screams not too far from Thormund's mansion. "Run," I told Cecelia, shoving her toward home. "Get inside, and lock your doors and windows." She nodded, her eyes wide with fear, and I watched her dart down the street. I pulled out my revolver and ran toward the sounds.

I could no longer hear the screams. As I rounded a corner, in the distance, I saw a few flashlights and what seemed to be a large group of people. I cautiously headed that way, walking very fast. As I got closer, out of the dark came out a familiar face.

"Luc! Our hero!" It was Jackson Thormund, and I instantly smelled trouble. "Come, come! You will love this!"

As he pulled me towards the group of men, to my horror, I saw that they had two young colored men and one white man tied up, with their mouths covered with rough fabric gags. The Klansmen were dragging them somewhere towards the hilly area of the city, closer to the ocean.

"That bastard," Jackson pointed at the white man. "He tried to fight us when we came for those two. Well, he can join them now."

My blood chilled as my heart began to pound uncontrollably with rage and terror as I finally saw where they were headed. There were several thick, tall wooden posts driven into the ground there, with black chains attached. Below each one was a pile of dry wood. *No, God! Please!* I could not watch this horror!

"Hey, what's with the crazy face? Don't get too excited now. I know you did a number on them at Kramik's, but tonight you can just watch," said Jackson, slapping me on the back.

I stood shaking and unable to speak. There was

nothing, nothing I could do to protect those three men. There were too many Klan members present, and quite a few had weapons.

They chained the three men to the posts. Several of the Klan members approached with torches.

God, please, please let them feel no pain, I prayed silently. Tears streamed down my face as the evildoers threw the torches onto the woodpiles and lit the men on fire. My senses became dull as my vision blurred, and I could barely hear anything. I turned and ran.

Once my senses returned, I found myself sitting by a brick wall. My head was throbbing. The Klan members were all gone, and only Jackson stood over me.

"I told you not to get too excited. You missed most of the show. Whaddaya mean, running off? I know you're not yellow, but some of my men aren't as tolerant as I am. I saved ya this time. If you act less crazy, next time, I'll let you torch them." He gave me a grim look and walked away.

Guilt and a sense of uselessness washed over me. I would die before allowing a "next time." I got up, and instead of going home, I headed to Kasp Nudd's place. I wanted to kill the Klan members, even if it cost me my life or the investigation.

My head continued throbbing as I walked into the rundown neighborhood again and passed through a dark alley. A trash can behind me rattled, and I started, drawing my revolver with a wobbling arm. It was just two street cats pillaging it. Their eyes lit up in the dark, and one hissed at me.

As I turned at the end of the second alley, intersected by a street, I saw a man in a white suit. My heart skipped a beat, and as I stepped forward, I heard a noise to my right. I looked that way and then quickly turned back to see the man, but as before, he was gone. I focused my attention on the strange noise on the right.

A weak streetlamp barely illuminated a brick wall, and I could see the shadow of creeping tentacles. Adrenaline rushed through my veins as I ran like lightning to Nudd's place. I banged on his door, and the moment he opened it, I fell inside, completely exhausted in every way.

I once again woke up, but this this time lying in a bed. It was early morning. The bed was small, and my feet were hanging off the end. I could see a window and several bookshelves. I felt my head. It was wrapped in bandages.

"Ah, the sleeping prince. Who bumped you on the head this time?" Kasp's voice came from behind the shelves, and his face peeked around them.

"Hey, it's just the first time...and I fell. I passed out. Here...sit for a moment."

Kasp sat down next to me, and I told him the whole story and then my plan.

"So...this is not your job, nor your business, but you decided to be some sort of vigilante. Okay...I like it." He patted me on the shoulder and left for a minute, then reappeared with some equipment and a very nice rifle. "I have two handguns, this rifle, and my knife. Is your revolver all you got?"

"No, I have other weapons at my apartment. I'm thinking another revolver and a shotgun."

"Good, good...we'll have to go at night, very late, kill as many as we can with knives, and shoot the rest. And you know the chance of making it out alive is pretty small, right?" Nudd's brows were raised in question.

"I will do this no matter what." My voice was thick with determination and conviction.

"Okay, no problem — you're getting as crazy as I am. It's good to have a friend with a similar mindset," he said, grinning ruefully.

This last comment disturbed me a bit, but he was close to the truth. I did feel like I was going crazy, but I also felt that this was the right thing to do. I had to do what I could to save the lives of innocent people, even if I failed Van Dausen's investigation and died.

Kasp advised me to nap for a while and gave me tea with a sleeping draught. Then he pulled blackout curtains over the windows. I finally relaxed and drifted off into sleep. I did not dream, and upon waking up, I nervously ran into Kasp's bathroom and began to tug at my face. I took out my small knife and cut my cheek. I felt a shot of pain as blood dripped down my chin and neck. I stared at myself in the mirror. How had I gotten this way so fast? Of course I wasn't a fake — it was my face. I was Luc Nistage. What was I thinking? I shook my head and walked out of the bathroom.

Kasp sat in the room in a rocking chair. He glanced at me. "Yeaaah...hmmm. Well...don't get too fired up now," he said calmly, with sarcasm in his voice. He was clearly enjoying watching me lose myself.

As I saw his reaction, I went back behind the bookshelves and prayed for a long time. I focused on my breath and on slowing my heartbeat. I became calm and still, regaining my normal train of thought. I returned to the bathroom, cleaned my cut, and sat down on the bed next to Kasp's rocker.

"Now that you're calm, you still want to do this?"

My spirit had regained its determination as well. I nodded firmly. "No one else will. There are not that many of them if both of us are well-armed and we surprise them. We just have to hope the neighbors don't see us flee the scene because the police will arrive shortly after the gunshots."

"Ah, I highly doubt it. Jackson is not a popular figure with the other wealthy in this city, and they control the police. If anything, they'll be happy he's in trouble."

"Let's hope you're right, Kasp."

CHAPTER ELEVEN

We went over to my apartment to wait. Night was coming, and I was starting to get very nervous. Kasp looked unchanged. His blood was as cold as a snake's.

He fixed me some coffee and told me to make my mind blank, to imagine infinite darkness. I struggled to do it, but it did slow my heartbeat a bit and improved my breathing.

"It's almost time," he said.

We had our weapons ready.

The street was dim and full of shadows as usual. We made our way into the dark alley right behind Jackson's mansion. The fence wasn't very tall, and we saw only one guard. They must have felt very safe in there. We speculated on how many actual members he did keep there for safety or other reasons.

My heart rate revved up again as I began to focus with all my strength. Kasp climbed the fence and waited for me behind a bush. He signaled for me to stay put. Then Kasp sneaked up behind the guard and used his knife to kill him. He dragged the body into the shrubbery.

We then proceeded to cautiously enter the large house through the back door, which was unlocked. It was silent inside and mostly dark, with just some light from the street lamps and the moon coming through the windows. We inspected the first floor and found just one man asleep on the sofa. Kasp quickly eliminated him.

Then came a voice. "Where is Bob? He'd better not be sleeping on duty again."

"You didn't see him through the window?" another man replied.

"No," said the first one.

"Should I go check?"

"Yeah, go slow, take this."

Kasp had moved silently into the shadows next to the stairway. A man came down the stairs quickly, making plenty of noise. He carried a shotgun. Kasp pounced on him and slit his throat, but just as the man fell, the shotgun went off, firing into the floor.

Next, we heard a great commotion and yelling on the upper floors. Two men were running down the stairs with guns. I fired at them with my shotgun as Kasp nailed one of them with his rifle.

"Into the room! Protect the wizard!"

We heard a door slam on the third floor as we slowly and silently crept up the stairs, guns at the ready. We reached the third floor, and there was a corridor to the left with just one door and a large window. That must be the room occupied by Jackson. All was quiet.

We waited several minutes. "There are two others in there with him," whispered Kasp. He used his handgun to fire at the doorknob.

The door opened a crack, and many shots followed, putting holes in the wall but not into us, as we had anticipated the thugs' reaction and stayed out of the way in the stairwell. Once the shots stopped, Kasp grabbed my shotgun and sprinted to the door, kicking it wide and firing the shotgun at the same time. Someone returned fire, hitting him in the arm, but he used his left hand to repeatedly fire his revolver. I ran up, ready to fire as well, but it was all almost over. The two men lay dead, with the third one, Jackson, standing in the center of the room looking shocked and holding his shoulder, which was bleeding. Kasp's right arm was also damaged and covered in blood, but he didn't seem to care as he approached Jackson.

Jackson gaped when he saw me. "You? Have you lost your mind, Luc? You want to become the wizard yourself? Why are you doing this?"

"Listen, Wizard...do a magic trick, and I'll let you go," said Kasp, and smiled.

"You'll pay for this...you won't get away with this!"

"Abracadabra," said Kasp, and fired a shot between Jackson's eyes. The KKK leader fell back, lifeless.

We set fire to all the curtains on the ground

floor and disappeared into the darkness. As Kasp had predicted, the authorities arrived much too late to save the building.

Kasp Nudd left me at my apartment and headed back to his place. He took my shotgun with him, saying he knew where to hide it well. I agreed and kept only my favorite revolver.

I lay in my bed, listening through my open window at all the commotion. Policemen, firemen, and neighbors came and went. While I was worried about being considered a suspect in the murders and arson, I couldn't help but feel satisfied that perhaps Nudd and I had saved more lives than we had taken and avenged the lives of many others.

Close to morning, I finally fell asleep, but it wasn't for long because of loud knocking on my door and someone yelling. I was sure it was the police as I wobbled over to open up. My head was heavy, and I could barely keep my eyes open.

To my surprise, at the doorstep stood Father Brannahan. When he saw me, he shoved a wad of money towards me.

"You lost this last time we met. I found it well after you left — lucky I did. I'm sorry for such an early intrusion, but it took a lot of effort to find where you live. I have to get going now to see to another event for the poor," he said, as he hurried down the steps. I stared at him in disbelief. Why had someone planted money on me?

"Um, how much is this?" I asked in a tired voice.

"How should I know, son? It belongs to you, does it not? I don't count another man's money. Remember, the Lord taught us not to desire what belongs to another man."

"Well, Father...as far as I know, the Lord also taught charity."

"Aye, that is correct."

I followed him down the steps and pressed the money into his hand. "Please use this money to help fund your projects for the poor and the church."

The bundle of money must have been more than a thousand dollars, but I felt this was the right thing to do. Brannahan thanked me incredulously, and I actually convinced him to come inside so I could shower and change and then to eat with me at the diner.

Bill approached us and seemed surprised to see me with a priest. He asked no questions about it, but he did ask something else.

"Have you heard yet?"

"About what, Bill?"

"Thormund Jackson and some of his people."

"No, what happened?"

"Didn't you wonder what was happening around here with all the noise last night? Anyhow, two things: First, three men were found and burned to death at the cliffs the night before. Then, last night, Thormund's house was lit on fire, and as far as I've heard, he is dead."

"Wow!"

I tried to show as much surprise as possible.

"Yes, retaliation." Bill grinned. "Anyway, you having the usual? How about you, Father?"

"I'll have the same he's having, whatever it is."

Bill walked away.

"I'm having waffles, eggs, and two coffees, Father."

"And that's just fine." The priest's eyes were dark with concern as he looked at me. "What are your feelings about this news? In your eyes, I could see no concern about Thormund's death. However, when that gentleman mentioned men at the cliff being burned, I saw a spark of anger in your eyes."

"Well, Jackson was a very, very bad man."

"And you believe someone took his punishment into his own hands?"

"Yes."

"And are you proud of that person?"

"I think so, yes."

Father Brannahan leaned back, his face calm and kind, but he was thinking. "I have often pondered this. How does God react to those who take the punishment of the wicked into their own hands? I came to one certain conclusion — that I know very little about this." Father Brannahan paused. "Perhaps it is God who drives those who punish the wicked. On the other hand, because He has granted us free will, God has no part in this sort of thing. But then, does He view it as wrong?" He shook his head. "I have read so much about various saints and people who have been chosen by God for specific tasks. It's not even about choosing someone good or wicked. God may choose bad men to do divine tasks as well, to become holy tools. 'Thou shall not kill.' But what about defending others from harm? If we see evil being done and do nothing about it, aren't we then part of that evil?"

I did not reply. I stared down at the wooden table and mulled over all that he said. It made me think deeply about my actions, but his refusal to pass judgement also made me feel better.

"Your face lightened up, Luc."

I looked up at him, and our eyes met. He stared deep into my soul, and I, without any shred of doubt, understood that he knew I was the one.

The priest smiled beatifically at me. "All you have to do is talk to God and understand that this life is your boat, not your island. Jesus knows our hearts. He knows that any sin can be cleansed. You must understand that each day is a new beginning. It's a new you. You don't have to cling to sins of the past and surely should not anticipate sins in the future. Today you tell yourself that you'll be the best you can be, and that's it. And tomorrow, you'll do the same. Continue learning and improving, and remember, God loves you."

Just then, our food arrived. Father enjoyed the meal greatly and said it was the best food he'd had in months. I was happy to hear that. I owed the man a lot. His words had given me relief and hope during my most difficult times. Once we finished, he went on his way, and I was ready to continue my investigation.

I picked up the morning newspaper, and of course, the latest events hadn't been reported yet. However, the most recent activity of the Night Hawk caught my eye. The story mentioned that several young women, who had not been identified, were victims. I scrambled to get to the police station to see if I could get more information.

Chapter Twelve

I took a trolley, which was half full. There was an old gentleman with the same newspaper in his hands. Two young men, who appeared to be coworkers, were sitting next to each other. Their faces and hands were rough, and I figured they didn't do an easy sort of work. I sat behind the older gentleman and relaxed into the seat. As we moved, I simply let my eyes watch outside without any particular focus. Everything smudged into a Monet like painting as I completely relaxed my eyes and tried to enjoy the ride. Every time we came to a stop, I closed my eyes.

When we arrived at my stop, I felt a bit more rested, and it was hard to get out quickly. Once outside, I moved my body around, loosening up my limbs and back. Despite the coffees, the inspirational words of the priest, and the soothing ride, I still knew that I needed much more rest to be able to perform at my full strength and intellectual capacity.

When I entered the station and asked for

Detective Willems, the young officer in the front informed me that Willems was indeed there, and he left to inform the detective. A minute later, he came back and invited me to go into the corridor behind him and find Willems's door.

It was a small police station. In the back, I could see the archives room. On the left were two offices and two cells, and on the right, there were two more offices. I saw the nameplate, which was old and in bad shape, with only the word "Detective" and no name. The door was cracked open, and I entered. The office was tiny and old, with peeling dark green paint. Behind a very messy desk sat Willems.

"Please sit, Luc. What brings you here? I suppose you heard about Jackson?"

"Yes, and thank you."

"Is that why you're here?"

"No, actually another matter."

Willems looked at me shrewdly. "You don't seem too disturbed about last night's events. Well, the less scum, the better. Anyway, what is it?"

"Well, here." I took out the article.

"What about it? More Night Hawk crimes."

"No, I mean the girls. Do you have anything on them? Any more information?"

"I have a few photos which we developed already, and here are my notes about the scene." He sat back and lit a cigarette.

Upon looking at the girls' photos, I realized that they all had similar legwear as the girl I had seen at Marie Toussant's house. Her girls had been killed, which meant she was not being careful with them at all. I had to go back to her and confront her about this.

"Thank you, Robert. I got what I needed."

"Wait." He exhaled a cloud of smoke and looked at me through narrowed eyes. "If you find anything suspicious, you let me know, okay?"

"Of course."

I took the first cab I could find. As I arrived in front of Marie's imposing house, a light rain began to fall. I knocked on the door and the same young woman as before answered. She was dressed exactly like the dead women in the photos: short dress, stockings, fancy garters. She invited me to wait inside on the first floor and showed me to a small room to the right of the entry, where there was a small red couch. The walls were red as well, and there was another couch, two coffee tables, and a globe on a marble stand. A large painting of a female nude hung over the fireplace.

I waited for about half an hour, then the girl came back, and I was taken to the same room as before, located on the third floor. Marie Toussant sat on the same couch with her feet on the glass table. Her green skirt was short, and her blouse was unbuttoned, revealing a great deal of her breasts. Around her neck were several pearl necklaces. She looked at me and laughed. On the table were empty wine glasses and a few bottles. I doubted whether she was sober, but was she ever?

"I just had company. He left, but now I have

more company," she trilled. She took out a little glass tube filled with cocaine, as before.

"Listen, Miss Toussant, this is important, please," I said, sitting down.

"What's important is that you take some of this first," she said, taking out the tiny spoon.

"No! Please, let me—"

"My house, my rules, young bull."

"Your girls were brutally murdered!"

Her expression changed slightly as she set the tube on the table. She regarded me silently, resentfully, for a moment or two. "So? Is that all?"

I couldn't believe her lack of concern. "What do you mean? That's a big deal! At least three of your girls have been murdered by Night Hawk! Who were their clients? Information you have could help find this murderer!"

"Help? Why should I help? People die, you know? My clients deserve privacy, and this is a business, just like any business. Sometimes products break or disappear, so you get new ones." Marie produced her long cigarette holder, placed a cigarette into the end, and lit it.

I was thunderstruck. "You are talking about human beings, with hearts, souls, blood, minds, dreams, just like you! They have a right to their lives. They are not products! Night Hawk should be stopped! And I don't believe you have no information about Aranxa Van Dausen!" Speech then failed me.

"Gee, thank you for killing my good mood." She

filled her wineglass and downed it in one go. "I don't care what you think. You can stay and have fun with me." Her voice turned coy. "Even though you're an asshole, you are handsome. I'll forgive your rudeness, but," then both her voice and her expression hardened again, "if you're not here for fun, get the hell out and never talk about my products or how I run my business to anyone."

Her eyes were devoid of any morals or kindness. She only knew lust, money, and pleasure. Sadness and intense dislike gripped me as I stood and stalked out.

It was pouring hard outside, but I walked a few blocks and got soaked before grabbing a taxi to get close to The Dark Turtle. I felt like drinking but didn't want to do it alone in my place. I greeted John and Maria and sat down by the window after ordering some cognac, which John told me was a rare and unusual bottle.

I watched the rain dimple the surface of the dark water of the canal, listening to its patter. I thought about the people I had spoken to. Everyone from a saint to a demon. I supposed each one of us, balancing on the rope of life, experienced the extremes. I sipped the cognac, and it was powerful. I felt fire in my chest, but it was exactly what I needed. I sat there for a long time, not inviting conversation with anyone. When the sun started to set, I left.

Upon my arrival home, I found two notes. One was from Mercedes, and the other was from Cecilia. The note from Mercedes said that Allard Van Dausen was in town and would like to see me tomorrow. The other note, from Cecilia, was an invitation to a party Mitch Stochild was hosting at his mansion, also tomorrow, but at night. I had bought the remainder of the bottle of cognac from John and brought it home with me. I sat by my window watching the street, which was now almost dark, with its single streetlamp.

For some reason, I recalled my childhood, and then it hit me. My father, Pierre Nistage, who had passed away when I was small, had always worn a white coat and hat. Chills ran down my spine as I gazed out the window and saw the man in white once again watching me from the shadows. Then he stepped into the dim pool of light around the lamppost and gazed up at my window.

It is my father! More chills ran down my back as tears welled in my eyes. How could it be? Was his spirit guarding me? Why had I been afraid before? Was he giving me a warning? Or perhaps it was just the effects of the alcohol.

I squeezed my eyes shut and let the tears fall, hanging my head. When I calmed down and looked out again, the street was empty. I strained to see, but there was no one there. Was I going crazy? It wouldn't have surprised me. I drank another glass of cognac, my vision blurred, and I staggered over to my bed and was soon asleep.

My sleep was disturbed again by visions and nightmares. Even as I slept, I was relieved and happy to have them because no matter how horrific they were, they meant that I was still myself.

I stood in the center of a street. It was long and paved in smooth, small black pebbles. On the sides of the street were buildings, also completely black. All their windows were shut. I began to walk. I heard a sound above me and looked up. The largest crow I had ever seen flew above me in the moonlight and landed on a street lamp, but this lamp's light was black as well. I went closer and looked at the crow. It, too, observed me with large black eyes burning with curiosity. It twisted its bird head right and left, examining me, and then it rapidly turned its head in the direction of the street and froze in that position. I looked into the distance and saw that the street had no end in sight. I continued walking, and in the dark windows of the black houses, white faces began to appear. I did not know these men, but then I recognized Jackson's face, silently screaming at me, and in another window, Charlie's face appeared, looking at me with sadness. To my left, I saw Kramik's face coldly gazing at me, and then on the corner of the street stood the man all in white. I could not see his face, but I assumed it was my father. The man turned away from me and began walking up the dark street. I followed him at the same pace. In the distance, I could see an outline of a giant throne appear and the ocean waves crashing against it. The man in white waded into the water and under the throne and disappeared into the ocean. One by one, out of the dark waters emerged long thin tentacles, dozens of them, followed by the body of a horrific creature resembling a spider and an octopus all at once. I was told without words that this was Sut Ni Tul.

I was paralyzed by horror and terror; I could not move. The fear was very real despite my realization that this was a nightmare. My legs wobbled, and I felt shooting pain through my lower back. My knees buckled, and I fell. As I was on my knees in pain, the tentacles of the creature approached me, and it opened two large eyes. They were blue orbs, and as I gazed into them, I was exposed to the deepest desires of the ancient creatures, the deep dwellers of the ocean. They did not come from our planet but from another place. Sut Ni Tul whispered into my ears, and what I heard chilled me to my bones.

As I woke up, I still felt the horror, but I could not recollect what Sut Ni Tul had whispered to me. I sat up in my bed and felt the chill of cold sweat on my back. This creature was real. I had seen it outside of the dream world, but now it was inside my head as well.

It was very early morning, and the sun was just starting to rise. Once I was able to shake off the feeling of terror and prayed, I felt a headache of monumental proportions. I stiffly got up and made coffee, and drank some water. As usual, I situated myself by the window and knew that today I had to face Van Dausen and tell him I still had no idea what had happened to his daughter. I had to be brave and confident and have faith, or so I told myself. I ate some cold ham and boiled eggs. I shaved, combed my hair, and put on nice clothes, but the dark bags under my eyes were unfortunately not removable.

CHAPTER THIRTEEN

I set out to meet with Allard at The Hook Hotel. The streets seemed less busy than usual, and when I got to the harbour, the waters were calm. There was a pleasant, light breeze coming from the ocean. I slowly walked by the water and then heard a familiar voice call out to me. It was Cecilia. She hurried up to me and gave me a strong hug.

"My dear Luc! Are you coming with me tonight to Mitch's party? Did you get my letter?"

"Yes, yes, of course I'll accompany you."

"Things in this town have been so crazy lately, even scary. Do you feel the same?"

I smiled at her, an oasis of beauty, calm, and happiness in a dark place. I took her hand and squeezed it. "Try not to fill your mind with fear. You are bright and beautiful, and today is a wonderful day. Everything will be all right."

"Thank you, Luc." She embraced me again, this time holding on a little longer. "Would you walk with me a while?"

"A little bit, but then I must report to my employer. He is in town."

She went onto a different subject. "Would you like to go out on a boat with me sometime?"

"I'd be delighted to. You love the water, don't you?"

"Yes! It makes me feel peaceful and calm, even when the waves are strong and high."

"It makes me wonder...."

"What does it make you wonder?"

"About life, about secrets hidden deep within those old waters."

She looked up at me, smiling and frowning at the same time. "Have you seen something? Your eyes lit up as you said that, Luc."

"I'm not sure, honestly. I'm not sure. It's just a feeling, nothing to worry about."

"Oh look, soda and coffee."

"Let's get some, and then I have to get going, sweet Cecilia."

We each got a bottle of soda and sat on the edge of the pier with our feet hanging off, and enjoyed chatting about the various things we saw. Afterwards, I hugged her tightly and headed to The Hook Hotel.

In front of the doors were now two men in black, who looked similar to the men I remembered Van Dausen having at our first meeting. Allard must have paid for security for the whole place while he was there. As I approached, they stopped me, but once I told them who I was, they immediately let me pass and told me to go to the end of the main hallway on the first floor.

As I entered the hotel, I was greeted by Mercedes, who sat in the lobby reading a book. I noticed it was Dante's *Inferno* as she set it aside.

"Cheery book there, Mercedes."

"A lot like this town?"

"Yes, very pleasant. How are you doing?"

"I'm in fine fettle, Luc. Mr. Van Dausen is waiting for you down the hall. Behind this building there is a restaurant called Bob's; it's well recommended. I think he wants to take you there to talk."

"Okay, thank you."

Just down the dimly lit hall was a circular room with dark green walls and a few paintings. A tired-looking Allard Van Dausen sat at a small table.

"Hello, Mr. Nistage."

He stood up and shook my hand as I greeted him. Then, as Mercedes predicted, he led me out a door and into the restaurant. It was a luxurious place with marble-topped tables, apricot-colored walls, and pretty light fixtures. No one was inside except for the manager and waiters. Only one table had place settings and menus on it. It was obvious that Allard had paid for a private meal just for us.

The table was by the window, overlooking the beautiful and mysterious ocean. We sat down, and Allard advised that we look at the menu first and order before we discussed the job.

Though it was fairly early in the day, my eyes instantly lit on the chestnut roast with mashed potatoes and fresh asparagus with hollandaise sauce. Allard, on the other hand, ordered a trio of lobster tails. The waiter thanked us and stepped away, and then brought us some fresh rolls with sweet butter and iced tea.

"So, Mercedes has kept me up to date, but it's been some time since your last report. I also will have you know that I have some of my men scouting the city now, asking questions as well. But before you get nervous, I want you to know that something deep inside of me still tells me that you'll find my daughter. I just hope she's alive." Allard turned away for a moment and wiped a tear from his right eye. "Any major news for me?"

"There are several people who remain prime suspects. What makes this difficult are a few specific factors."

"Such as?" Van Dausen fixed me with a penetrating gaze.

"These people are liars, are highly immoral, nothing they say can be trusted, and they feel completely above the law. I will have to stake out and keep watch on one of them for the next several nights and days, maybe longer, because, at this point, I feel that could lead me to something."

"Whom will you be spying on, then?"

"Mitch Stochild."

Allard's mouth was set in a thin line. After a few beats, he spoke. "He is the man who runs this city, and he has more influence than anyone. Mercedes said you found out something disturbing about him, but she said that details were better left for you to describe."

I took a deep breath and a swallow of the tea. "Mitch is a leader of a cult in these parts. They perform very disturbing rituals."

"And you believe Aranxa could have been a victim of this cult?"

"Yes, absolutely, but I need more evidence. There is nothing concrete. She might not be connected to Mitch or the cult in the end. It is very complicated. I've never dreamed that such a place as this existed. To describe it as corrupt and upside down would be a great understatement."

Van Dausen sighed. "I've read some more about this. The Night Hawk—I shudder at the thought that she could have been his victim as well. What do you think? Why is it taking this city so long to stop this killer?"

"Because he provides cover for the big fish and creates chaos and fear. Once the public is in fear, it's easy to manipulate them, control them, and squeeze all the money out of them. The police department is corrupt to the core here, and the city isn't seeking help from the outside. There is just one honest detective on this case."

"Luc, I'll be completely honest with you. This cannot drag on for too much longer. I will want more answers soon. Each day is agonizing mental and spiritual torture."

I thought of suggesting that he meet with Father Brannahan but realized that this comment could be viewed as insensitive. "Of course, Mr. Van Dausen. I will have the results soon. I feel I am close to the end of all this. My next step might lead me to a big discovery."

"I sure hope so."

Our meals came, cooked to perfection, but still not as tasty as the food I'd had at Stochild's mansion. When we finished our dessert and coffee, I waited for Allard to excuse me. He sat a long time, staring into the ocean, his eyes filled with sadness. I could feel that hope was draining from him. A seagull landed near the window, and it brought him back to reality. He turned to me and nodded. I thanked him and left with a heavy heart. All the pressure on me had just intensified, and even though he did not seem violently inclined, if I were to fail, I knew that behind his calm mask was another man, one who was ruthless. After all, it was his daughter, and he had given me an incredible amount of money.

I went back to my apartment for a bit, just killing time. At this point, I was putting all of my eggs in one basket, and if Mitch wasn't going to lead me to the revelation of this mystery, I wasn't confident that anyone or anything else would. I went to Heavenly Diner for a cup of coffee. The street outside was quite busy, and through the window, I could see workers clearing the mess from the burned mansion of Jackson Thormund.

Then I felt a tap on my shoulder and heard a

familiar voice. I turned, surprised. It was Kasp Nudd.

"I saw you from the street. You always glued to the windows like this?"

"I suppose." I shrugged. "Please have a seat. I'll get you something."

"Sure, sure, just a coffee will do just fine. I am picking up some nice rare books from a scholar that lives around here, so that's why I'm here."

Bill stepped over, and Kasp made his order.

"Have you heard of Roland Garros?" he said, folding his arms on the table.

I shook my head.

"Ah, well, he was a hero for the French during the war. I met him. I lived in France before the war started, you know, and during...sort of...well, more like all over the place at that point, fighting. Anyway, there is some argument as to whether Roland was the first ace pilot. Some claim he shot down more than five planes, but most say it was four."

"Oh." I had no idea what he was talking about.

"Well, like I said, I met him. He was an ace all right—fearless, the fire of freedom in his eyes. People used to say I had the same eyes, but by the end of the war, people were telling me I had bloodlust eyes. Strange how that works."

"Terrible events change us."

"Any! Any events change us! There are good, bad, and in between, but every event changes us, at least a little bit." He leaned in closer to whisper, "Like what you did with me, it changed you, yeah? What affected you more, seeing those Klansmen burn their victims or getting revenge on them? Playing the judge and jury, yeah?"

"I don't know, Kasp. It all...brought pain into my soul, into my heart. I'm not sure it changed me, but it made me understand the world better."

Kasp slapped the table. "That is change, my friend. Revelations of reality. Revelations of cruelty and suffering. Ah, good, good coffee. Damn good coffee," he said abruptly as Bill put the cup in front of him. He left the pot on the table.

I decided to change the subject. "Sure, so what kind of books?"

"Actually, old books about cults and clans, medieval pagans, that sort of thing."

"What do you think about those times? Burning the witches and all?" I sipped from my own coffee cup.

"I think a lot of things. Those times weren't just savage times, my friend. Many great minds lived during those times as well. And you know, pagans used to steal Christian children and sacrifice them in their demon worship. I don't feel bad for them getting eradicated, but I do want to learn more."

"How old do you think are the cult's origins in this area?"

"Origins? The root of it?" Nudd frowned, staring into his coffee cup. "As old as the human world, because the root of it is human nature. Some fall for the charms while others don't. You know?" Kasp finished his second coffee and stood up. "You be careful now,

Luc. Remember, you come to me if you're in danger. I will help you."

"Thank you, Kasp. See you around."

After he left the diner, I looked down into my coffee cup. The black grounds on the very bottom created the shape of octopus tentacles. I shook my head and quickly refilled the cup. As I poured, I thought I saw a blackbird sitting on the side of the table. Was my mind completely slipping?

I decided to visit a couple of places I hadn't paid much attention to before. One of them was the largest park in the town, which had been a beautiful old square, not far from the city hall. As I had before, I got on a trolley and took a newspaper with me.

There were stories about power outages in the north part of the town, a new election coming up, and an interview with an actor, but this time surprisingly, there was no article about the Night Hawk. I was aware that many believed the Night Hawk also kidnapped his victims or hid their bodies, so the lack of news did not mean the murders had slowed down, although one could hope. Perhaps he'd slipped, fallen, and died. How would that be? No one would ever know. Like Jack the Ripper, all would think the Night Hawk had simply gotten away with it or moved to another city.

When I arrived at the park, I was pleased to see the abundance of trees and noticed that the air had a scent of freshness. The colors around me were vibrant. A better-maintained section of the canal flowed through here. I meandered down to a path. Just on my left near the water sat two pretty young women, laughing and enjoying their day. On my right, a small boy was running back and forth between his mom and dad, his eyes sparkling with joy. That was the right kind of childhood; normalcy and love were blessings. I could not remember much of my own childhood. I sat on a bench and listened to the birds sing wonderfully. The laughter of the boy and the young women made me feel happier somehow. I felt that even if I felt despairing, there was still much joy and love in the world around me.

Suddenly my mind shifted to thinking about Night Hawk. I felt a need or the urge to punish whoever he was. How much laughter and joy had this person stolen from families like this one?

I knew the strong emotions I felt about the injustice here were my enemy. Then I thought of Charlie. Had killing the new version of him been an evil deed as well? Was I, too, a part of the town's dark side? Or was I on a fool's errand, trying to light a candle in the darkest spot in a secretive, evil place?

What I really needed to do was focus my mind and energy on one person only: Aranxa.

I got up and took a half-hour stroll by the water, thinking some more. I decided I would start watching Mitch tonight, right after his party. I watched a little bird by the water grab a small worm just before another one did. From up above, I heard several other birds chirp, probably indicating their desire to find some food as well. I noticed a little tunnel up ahead of me with many green bushes around it. I was curious to see what was on the other side. As I walked through it, I followed the light at the other end. It felt poetic, walking towards it out of the dark. Once I emerged, I found a small garden with statuary all around it. So, this was the artist's garden I had read about in one of the newspaper columns.

One of them caught my eye in particular. It stood by the water. It was a statue of a woman in a long dress. She was removing a mask from her face with her right hand. Half of her face was still masked, the other revealed. I looked down and read the name of the artist.

"Graham Stochild."

Surely this had been done a long time ago by a relative of Mitch. Was the family already involved with the creature even before Mitch became an adult? The date on the statue was 1880, more than forty years ago. Why was I so surprised? The roots had to be deep to create a strong tradition and to build influence. It was like a big tree. From a tiny seedling grows strong roots, and then the tree grows and spreads, creating other trees as well. Such was the nature of many things in nature and many schemes of man. Education, medicine, science, politics, business, cults and clans, religion. From the seed came the roots, and then the rest was built. So, how important was it that the seed was planted with love and goodness rather than something else? Absolutely crucial. Like the seed planted by Christ against the seed planted by Satan.

It is easier to give in to evil rather than to strive to be good, noble, and honorable, kind and loving. Spreading the seeds of evil is easy because men constantly face sorrow, and to deal with these harsh realities with faith and hope is harder than to simply give in to blame, fear and anger.

I left the statue garden back through the tunnel. As I came back into the first area, I saw new people there; a few friends near the bench talking and a young couple sitting where the two young women had been before.

I decided to walk back to my place, and it took a long time. It was almost sunset when I reached my apartment and realized that I had to get ready quickly for the party.

As I was getting dressed, I noticed a whiskey bottle sitting on the table. For the first time in my life, I felt disgust towards it. The feeling came almost as a shock to me. I picked it up and held it, looking at it thoughtfully. I had no desire to drink it at all. I wondered what had caused this sudden change. Was it my thoughts about spirituality and understanding of Father Brannahan's words? Perhaps it was my subconscious that had evolved and was trying to lead me to a better path, one that would give me more clarity.

I finished putting on my black suit and went over to Cecilia's. The moment she opened the door, I was stunned by her beauty. She looked even more lovely than usual. She wore a silky white dress and long white gloves. A diamond clip glittered in her hair, and she held a white fox wrap. Her eyes were shining as she smiled up at me.

We took a cab to Mitch Stochild's mansion and were greeted there by a servant, who led us inside. There were already many people there. A long buffet table held all sorts of food. Waiters were passing around drinks. Many guests held glasses of wine. There was laughter and chatter in the air. In the background, a jazz band could be heard playing a soft, low tune.

I immediately felt uncomfortable, like a fish out of water. Everyone here behaved in a way foreign to me. It was—fake. Fake attitudes, fake smiles, fake happiness.

Then I noticed Mitch. I realized that he indeed was a standout. As evil as I knew him to be, he was the special one, the one who drew these weak-spirited sheep toward him. Throughout history, men like him had the ability to do either great good or great evil. Some believed they were doing good, while their acts were viewed by most as evil. Was Mitch a believer in his own actions? Did he view himself as good?

He noticed us and approached. "Dear, dear lovely couple. Two such splendid young flowers together— Oh, perhaps being referred to as a flower offends you, Luc?"

"Not at all, Mitch," I smiled. Fake. "How are you tonight? The party looks...fun."

"Hmm, I can tell you are not a great admirer of such gatherings, but they are good! Good for me at least, and good for your stomach, no?" He pointed at the table.

"Oh Mitch, this is really wonderful!" said Cecilia, bubbling with enthusiasm.

"Thank you, my dear. Well, I have to greet many other guests, but you go ahead and enjoy the festivities." He wandered away, glad-handing and greeting the sycophants he passed.

As the night went on and we ate and danced, I avoided alcohol and only drank tea. I kept my eyes on Mitch as much as I could without neglecting Cecilia, but nothing appeared to be amiss. The only strange thing I noticed was when a young woman and several men approached the back wall behind the band. Mitch met them, and they all disappeared into a hallway. After some time, the men re-emerged and left. A few minutes later, Mitch also reappeared, but I never saw the young woman again. For the rest of the night, I watched for her, to no avail.

When the party began to dwindle, Cecilia, who had imbibed quite a bit, and I took a cab back to our apartment building. On the way home, she fell asleep leaning against me. This was an uncomfortable situation for me, as I felt awkward carrying her into her apartment when she had not actually invited me in. Once inside, I laid her gently on the sofa in the living room. I dared not search for her bedroom with her in such a state. I covered her with a warm wool blanket I found in a basket near the fireplace, left the keys on the side table, and left.

But my night was far from over. Immediately I got back into the cab. So the driver wouldn't get suspicious, I had him drop me a few blocks away from Mitch's mansion, right by the water. From there, I walked to the mansion, staying close to the water. I found a small dock with what I figured was Stochild's yacht firmly tied to it and hid among some large boulders by the water, wondering about that young woman.

Once everyone had left the party, I understood that I had been right to follow my gut feeling. Two men came down the steps that led to the mansion, went aboard the yacht, and began to prepare it for sailing. Shortly after, they went back up to the house, and to my horror and sadness, when they returned, they were walking the blindfolded young woman to the boat with her hands tied behind her. Right behind them was Mitch, following with confident strides.

I had to act quickly. Desperately I peered around and noticed a boat tied to a floating dock farther down the shoreline. I knew it was a crime to take someone's rowboat, but I had to see this through. I managed to get over to it in the darkness and cut the rope.

Mitch's craft had set sail, surely towards the island. I began to row the boat using all of my strength. Adrenaline and the firm conviction that I had to carry out justice filled me with a righteous furor.

The waves were rough but manageable. I pushed and pulled the oars rhythmically and made sure to pace myself. The ship was getting away, but I followed its light, and when they reached the island, I could still see them in the distance.

I had to find a place to hide the boat and cut through the undergrowth so any guards on Mitch's boat would not see me. By the time I found a likely spot, my muscles felt like they were on fire, but so was my heart, filled with a powerful mix of terror and courage. I took out my revolver and silently made my way through the trees and the bushes, finding the cave entrance once again. I could see the ship from there, and indeed both guards had remained on it, which meant Mitch had taken the girl inside by himself.

I walked through the cold and dark cave, carefully shielding my flashlight and sliding along the wall, trying to not make any loud sounds. Suddenly I heard a piercing scream, cut short. I sped up my pace to reach the large chamber.

When I got there, the torches were lit, and I could see that the chair in front of the black hole was covered in blood. There was no creature and no girl. It must have taken her. In front of the chair was Mitch, kneeling on the ground and surrounded by candles. I pointed my revolver at him and slowly approached. He felt my presence and turned his head. His eyes got large as he saw me, and he stood up.

"Luc? What are you doing here, my young friend?"

"I know who you are...I know who you *really* are."

"And who's that?"

"You are the cult leader, worshipping that... thing...a demon, a monster. What did you do to that girl?"

"Oh my, oh my. Calm down, Luc, I'm not your enemy! Look, it's an ancient being. You are smart. You can understand. He is wise beyond humans, but he needs to feed on memories, and sometimes on flesh, too."

"You sick bastard," I spat. "Is that what you did to Aranxa Van Dausen?"

"Hahaha, oh, no, no...Luc." He approached with open arms.

"Don't move again!!!"

He stopped and smiled at me, confident and charismatic as ever. "Luc, a young man already with such a pained soul and hurting heart! I can take it all away, and all you will feel is bliss, I promise you."

"Stay away, you murderer." I held the gun with both hands, pointed straight at his head.

"Hah, Luc. That's ironic, coming from a man running around town with the Night Hawk."

"What??"

"Luc, you are a good investigator, but your experiences here have clouded your mind. Kasp Nudd is the Night Hawk! That wasn't obvious to you?" He shook his head. "You think I don't know? You think it's normal the way he enjoys the killing and how he kills?"

My mind went to the image of Kasp squeezing out Kramik's eyes. Cold sweat appeared on my forehead. Could it be true?

"Now, lower your weapon and come to me. You will feel you're in paradise! You came to a city called Paradise Harbour, and indeed I can give you that! You will be my apprentice after your magnificent transformation!"

As he spread his arms wider, I shot him twice in the chest. When he fell, I walked up to his body and shot him in the head to make sure he was gone. Then I ran as fast as I could out of that evil place. As I came out of the cave, the two guards were swiftly approaching the entrance. I locked eyes with one of them before I ran into the darkness among the trees.

Rowing back through the dark waters, I expected the ship to chase me down, but it never happened. I guessed that perhaps the henchmen were probably in shock, having found their beloved leader dead. When I reached the shore, I was completely exhausted, but instead of heading home, I decided to go somewhere else. I simply had to know. I had to check. I headed towards Kasp Nudd's house.

The streets were dark, and a dense fog was setting in. Despite this being an atmosphere that could seem dangerous, I actually felt comfortable. The fog added to the dark night meant it would be unlikely I'd be seen. I had learned the best shortcuts to get to Kasp's store and home, so it took me only about an hour to get there.

I stayed hidden in a doorway nearby and watched Nudd's door and the street for a while. There was no movement. Then I swiftly walked across and gently tried the door. It was locked, but I picked the lock and quietly opened the door.

I got inside and pressed my back against the wall. First, I ever so slowly and cautiously checked the bookstore. It was dark, and no one was there. I proceeded through the door in the back and into Kasp's actual home. I stood by the stairs listening, and as I began to ascend, I noticed a faint glimmer of light coming from the slightly opened basement door. I crept back down and put my ear to the crack and heard a sawing sound. I ducked inside the door, and with my revolver ready, I went down the stairs at a snail-like pace.

As I reached the bottom of the steps, a horror even greater than that I'd experienced with the cult greeted me. The walls of the basement were covered with human bones and skulls. There were shelves with bottles of preserved body parts and organs. On the floor lay what looked like a stack of human skins. I could see the letter Z carved into the top one.

Over in a corner, Kasp was leaning over a table, cutting something, with his back to me.

At that moment, Kasp Nudd turned around. He held a small saw in his hands and an arm in another, and when he saw me, he placed both of those back on the table. His face was calm. With my hand trembling, I raised my revolver and pointed it at him.

"What...and why...?" I could barely force myself to speak. This man had saved my life. Without him, I'd have been dead for days.

Kasp smiled faintly. "Why not, Luc? Don't look so sad! These are just..." he gestured around the room, "...people."

"People with their own lives, dreams, hopes, families, free will!" I shook my head as if by doing so, I could get rid of the horror in this room.

"Ah, yes. Well, I suppose I am a very ill man." He held up his hands in surrender. "You can kill me. I don't mind."

He stood still, without moving, his gaze relaxed and steady. I could tell he was serious.

"Why don't you stop? Will you kill again, or will you stop?"

"Oh, I will surely kill again."

My hand kept trembling as I tried to aim. Kasp stood there without moving a muscle. There was only one thing to do. With all the courage I had left, I pulled the trigger. The hit was directly between his eyes.

I sat back on the steps, sobbing. Only one thought swirled in my mind. Even if I survived all of this in the end, how badly would my mind be damaged for the rest of my life? All that money—it wasn't worth it.

Nevertheless, I promised myself that I'd see the case to the end. I left that basement of unspeakable horrors and headed out to find Willems.

CHAPTER FOURTEEN

When I reached the police station, I had calmed down considerably, but I also insisted that Willems be called in. Fortunately, the young officer at the desk decided not to argue, and after twenty minutes or so, Willems showed up, obviously having dressed in a hurry.

We sat in the messy office, and Willems looked at me resentfully and wearily. But once I began my story, be grew more and more alert, and he insisted that I take him to Nudd's horrible lair.

Tears rolled down the hardened cop's face as he took in what Nudd had done. I made him swear to take all the credit and leave me out of the story. He shook his head but agreed. Finally, I headed home. Once I was well away from Nudd's part of town, I found a cab and went to my apartment, just as the sun began to rise.

The next day a special edition of the paper shouted the end to the murders. Detective Willems's name was on everyone's lips. He was the hero. The town took a big sigh of relief that day.

As for me, I slept for several hours, then got up and showered and changed. I knocked on Cecilia's door to find out how she was feeling, but she was not home. I spent most of the day sitting in my room, feeling empty and drained.

As the evening drew near, I was able to bring myself back to reality, and I headed to the Ferry Cafe for what I figured was my final trip there. I walked slowly as I felt my being unimaginably depleted. The only thing that kept me going was the inspiration sparked by Father Brannahan to find my own voice of faith and hope deep inside my soul. It gave me the determination to look for a way forward no matter what was going on or happening inside or around me. Whatever it was, even though I felt drained, I knew I had to see this mission through to the end.

I flagged down an older driver with grey hair and a full beard who was offering his services as a driver and got in the car.

I leaned back into the seat as I sat in the man's car. He was very humbly dressed, his hands wrinkled and rough, his face exhausted, and his shoes had holes in them, so even before we set off, I gave him a decent amount of cash. His eyes got big as he stared at me with disbelief. I simply patted him on the shoulder and told him where I wanted to go.

The old man eyed me in the rearview mirror, then spoke. "Young man, you have such a kind heart, but why are your eyes so sad? Why is your spirit low? Aren't you doing God's work by helping men like me? God blesses you."

"Yes, I suppose He does," I answered wearily.

As I got out of the car, it began to rain. Luckily I was inside in a minute. The hostess, Silvia, knew me and took me to the table where Cecilia and I always sat, except I was alone this time. I sat back in the comfortable chair as a sparkling drink was brought to me. The lights were already dimmed, for I had missed the first performer, but Bryan, one of my favorites, was up next. He came out onto the stage in a nice brown suit, with perfectly combed hair and a slight smile on his face. The crowd applauded as he sat on a tall stool with the band situated right behind him.

"The princess in the sky
Smiles so gently
But she's only a cloud.
I know that I'm dreaming.

Yet it's her smile
That fills all my dreams.
Maybe one day
Life will be all that it seems.

The sun and the moon
Their laughter and tears,
They'll bless me together
I'll forget all my fears.

The morning is shining,
Her laughter's in my ears.
So sweet and romantic.
But it all disappears.

At night a reflection
Of stars in a pond.
I sing my complexion
A sorrowful song.

The sun and the moon
Their laughter and tears
They'll bless me together
I'll forget all my fears

All that's left is to dream
To trust that it's real.
Forget all the pain
It's love that I feel.

Forget all my sorrow
She'll always be there.
Sweet song of tomorrow
But today's where I stay."

Bryan's voice was soothing and soft, and I let one song after another wash over me. I felt my face relax and soften, my jaw loosened, and I realized how tightly I had been clenching it for so long. Even my hands lay flat on the table.

I allowed myself to dream of taking Cecelia and leaving Paradise Harbour, but just as the song said, it was only a dream, for I still had to finish my task. But for now, I allowed myself to live in the moment where dreams were possibilities, and the music lifted me up and out of my troubles.

After the last performer finished his set, I still sat there waiting to be the last one to leave the cafe. Bryan stepped up onto the stage and picked up some sheets of music he'd left on top of the piano. He noticed me and looked surprised I was still around.

"God bless you, sir," he said to me before stepping out the door.

I followed shortly. The rain had stopped, and it was rather cold. The light of streetlamps reflected in the puddles. A chilly breeze was coming from the ocean. I slowly walked along the streets, not really paying attention to my surroundings as I usually would. A black cat came from an alley. His paws were wet, and he stopped between the puddles to stare at me. I searched my pockets for something to give to him, but couldn't find anything.

"Sorry, buddy, got nothing for you." The cat streaked away.

I had meandered off the main street and decided to stop strolling aimlessly and make my way back to where I might find a taxi. I stopped to get my bearings and heard movement behind me. I turned but saw no one. The hairs on my neck were standing up, and I knew I was being followed. I turned down a side street, walking quickly and looking behind me. Footsteps echoed behind me, and I turned to face my stalker, pulling my revolver as I did so.

Several hooded figures were coming toward me at a run. One held a knife, another a rope. In horror, I realized that these people were cult members, bent on revenge!

I fired at the one with the knife and ducked around a corner. The knife-wielder was down, but the rest of them were still coming after me. I fired four more times, and then I ran up a flight of stairs. They led to another alley, and the streetlight there was partially out. I hid in the shadows of some garbage cans and quickly reloaded my revolver, waiting for them to appear.

The moon broke from behind the clouds, and I saw them clearly: three hooded people, two with knives, and I could not see if the third had a weapon. I aimed, and it all happened very quickly.

I fired at the two cultists with the knives, hitting one in the chest and the other in the head. Then the third raised a hand toward me, and I fired several more shots, emptying my gun. I sat there breathing heavily as I reloaded again, in case more cultists were coming. I waited for a minute, two, then three, then five, but there were no more sounds.

Cautiously I got up and moved toward the bodies, my gun at the ready. It was clear by the pools of blood under them that I wouldn't need it.

I removed the hoods from the first two cultists, both young men who looked to be in their twenties. But when I pushed back the hood from the third body, my heart leaped in shock. It was Cecelia.

I choked back a sob and looked away. I'd been such a fool! How had I not seen it? She had been so friendly with Mitch, admired him — and she'd worn the octopus ring. Tears dripped down my face as I looked at her eyes that would never open again, her lips that would never smile again.

But then I noticed something. The skin of her face seemed to melt and wrinkle, as Charlie's had. Reluctantly I pulled at the mask skin. It came away in my hand. Beneath it was a different face, one that was strangely familiar to me but that I could not quite place. "Oh no. It couldn't be," I muttered. I frantically searched the inside pockets of my coat for Aranxa's picture.

Yes. The dead girl was Aranxa. She had been one of the brainwashed! The earnest, brilliant medical student who had come to this place seeking knowledge and happiness had instead found its counterfeit. I let go of the photo, and it gently floated down to land next to the dead girl's face.

Indeed it was Allard's daughter. The girl I had come here for, the one I had endured all this madness for, was the one I had just killed. I sat back against the wall and hung my head, staring at the ground. The investigation was over. How was I supposed to explain this to Allard? I could barely comprehend it myself.

His daughter had been with me this whole time.

How could I have known humans were capable of such terrifying and demonic actions? Every ancient myth took on the possibility of fact after what I had seen. And no one would believe me. I recalled Mercedes' reaction as I had told her some of the things I'd learned. She already thought I was heading toward madness. Surely Allard would either kill me or put me in an asylum. No financial reward was worth this. I wished with all my heart that I could turn back time and say no to Van Dausen's offer, but nothing could change things now. These terrifying, unbelievable experiences were all part of me now, deeply entrenched in my mind and psyche.

Well, I certainly could not stay here. I got up and covered the heads of the bodies with their hoods once again. I hesitated when I came to Aranxa. I picked up the picture and briefly entertained the idea of taking her body out into the ocean or to the island, but I couldn't do it. I felt guilty just leaving her lying there, but I gathered the strength to do that and walked away.

I lay in my apartment on the floor almost the whole day, without eating or drinking. When I saw the sun begin to weaken, I went outside and walked in the direction of the small church on the cliffs.

I had known I'd be back in that spot again. I stood at the lighthouse near the cliffs. The dark waters of the powerful ocean crashed against the rocks, violently, beautifully, time and time again. The sun was gently setting, and I wondered what the next wave of my life would bring. Was there going to be a new dawn for me, or did I have just the dusk remaining?

The End.

Alexander Semenyuk (also known as Oleksandr Semenyuk) is a Ukrainian-American author. He was born in Lutsk, Ukraine, in 1986. At 14, he immigrated to the United States. Alexander's favorite genres are sci-fi, horror and fantasy. Early in life, Alexander was greatly influenced by classic literature and, since childhood, dreamed of becoming a writer.

Made in the USA
Monee, IL
30 October 2021